Hughes, Monica, 1925–.   ' 03131
    The dream catcher / Monica Hughes. -- Toronto :
Methuen, c1986.
    171 p. ; 22 cm.

03044696   ISBN: 0458807206 :

I. Title.

D1268951

6857 LSCB   87JUN25 06 /903-67027273
PRODUCED IN CANADA BY UTLAS int.   PRODUIT AU CANADA PAR UTLAS int.

+ 2 cop

The Dream Catcher

MONICA HUGHES

The Dream Catcher

 *METHUEN*

Toronto   New York   London   Sydney   Auckland

Canadian Cataloguing in Publication Data

Hughes, Monica, 1925–
The dream catcher

ISBN 0-458-80720-6

I. Title.

PS8565.U43D73 1987   jC813'.54   C86-094799-8
PZ7.H83Dr   1987

Printed and bound in the U.S.A.

1 2 3 4   87   91 91 89 88

Contents

1
The Tyranny of the Web

THREE FLOORS below ground, at eleven-thirty on a fine August morning, school was in session. It was Web Practice time, and in each classroom the students sat silently concentrating, eyes closed, minds reaching out to connect. Each person connecting to the next, each classroom with the other, until every neophyte and adult in Ark Three was linked. The energy level rose. The City hummed with a silent psychic hum.

Beyond the dome that enclosed the City a light breeze tossed a meadowful of flowers. A skylark sang in the intensely blue sky. A bumblebee clambered clumsily into the throat of a columbine, searching for nectar. It backed up, dusty with pollen, and flew on a zigzag course to another flower.

Buzz! Buzz! Right in her ear. Ruth squeaked and her eyes flew open. For a moment it seemed to her that she had been Outside. Then she saw the rows of girls, each with folded hands and obediently closed eyes. Bother! I've done it again! She squeezed her eyes shut and tried to empty her mind of everything except her connection with the minds of the girls on either side of her.

"All right, students. Eyes open. Stretch . . . and now relax. Let's see how we did." Teacher Jonson bent over the inked record that spilled out of the potentiometer on her desk. She tore the paper free and held it up for them to see.

A smoothly pulsating line – with a sudden jagged break in it like a spike on a fever chart.

7

"Ruth again, wouldn't you know?" Angela muttered. Charity groaned and rolled her eyes up.

"Quiet, please. Ruth, *was* it you?"

Ruth's cheeks grew hot. She stared at the plastic top of her desk until it went out of focus and shimmered. "I'm sorry," she muttered.

Teacher Jonson sighed. "All right. What was it *this* time?"

"I'm not sure. But it was beautiful. Green and moving colours and a golden light. Sunshine, I think. Then something buzzed in my ear and I jumped. But it was so real . . ." She looked at Angela, sitting in the desk next to her.

"Well, it certainly wasn't *me*," said Angela virtuously. "I was paying attention to Web Practice."

"That's enough. Class dismissed. No, Ruth, not you."

Ruth sank back into her desk and clenched her hands in her lap. Not another row! There had been so many in the last year that she had almost forgotten what it was to be ordinary and unnoticed. But it wasn't my fault, she thought. I do try. I really do. Oh, I wish I were like Patience. She can link her mind to anyone in the Ark, just like that. She'll become a Communicator on New Year's Day, that's certain. Or Faith. Her touch makes you feel better right away. She's sure to be a Healer. Oh, they are lucky to know who they are.

She spread her own hands in front of her, clumsy square-tipped hands, the nails bitten, the cuticles ragged at the edges. Even her hands were awful. What could be worse than being the dumbest kid ever to be born in Ark Three?

"Ruth, do pay attention!"

She jumped and hid her hands in her lap. "Sorry, Teacher Jonson."

"My dear, don't look so miserably guilty. I know you don't wander on purpose. I just wish we could get to the bottom of *why*. It's not easy to form a perfect Web. We've all had to learn, even the Protector. Many times there have been messages so powerful that they broke through an individual's concentration. But there has always been a good reason: the

8

call for a Healer, for instance. Your distractions seem so . . . well, so trivial. Colours and sunshine and something buzzing! Do you remember what it was last time?"

"Oh, yes. I was lying on my back somewhere Outside, watching cloud patterns. Then a bird flew by and its shadow made me jump."

"And the time before?"

"I was among trees, big dark ones, not like the trees we can see from the Dome. It was horribly spooky."

"And in the last two years there has been no hint of your future strength? Do you see yourself as becoming a Healer? A Communicator? A Teacher?" Ruth shook her head dumbly. "Dear me, it is difficult, isn't it? I don't remember when we've had a student quite like you. When is your fifteenth birthday?"

"September the twenty-third, Teacher Jonson."

"And less than five months to the New Year. Well, we'll have to try a little harder, won't we? Fight these distractions. Tell yourself that they are only your imagination, that they have nothing whatever to do with the Ark."

"Yes, Teacher Jonson," Ruth answered meekly, though she wanted to shout that they *were* real, that her daydreams were far more important to her than anything that happened in Ark Three.

"Off you go to lunch. Try not to worry. It'll come out right in the end. You'll probably grow out of it."

But I don't really want to, thought Ruth. If only it didn't interfere with the Web. Oh, why does life have to be so complicated? She disentangled her long thin legs from her desk, tripped over her feet in the aisle and scurried out of the room.

She was going to be late for lunch, but if she skipped washing and hair-tidying she might catch up. She pushed past a bunch of Grade Fivers in the main corridor and caught up with Grade Eight C at the door of the big dining room. How tidy they all were. She smoothed down her wiry hair with her hands and noticed an ink mark on her finger.

9

As she sucked at it guiltily she heard Angela's clear voice from the line ahead. "Our average is lower than any Grade Eight's since the beginning of the Ark, I bet. And it's all *her* fault. I wish she was in another class."

"Have you thought about New Year's Day?" She heard Faith answer. "We won't be neophytes any more. We'll be out of the dormitory and into our own rooms."

"So?"

"Three of us are going to have to room with *her*."

"Well, it's certainly not going to be me!"

"Nor me! Why can't she behave normally, like the rest of us?"

Ruth stopped and let the crowd push past her. Then she turned and ran back to the central elevators. One stood open and empty. She jumped in and pushed the 'Close' button quickly and kept her finger on it while she made up her mind where to go. There weren't many places where a person could be alone. Being together in a group was what Ark Three was all about, what the Web was about. And she had to be alone. That was one of the things that made her so different.

She could leave the elevator and go to the dormitory, but someone was sure to find her there. The library was a possibility, but there might be boys working in the library and she would die if a boy were to see her with her face like this. She made up her mind and pressed the 'G' button. The elevator rose to ground level and the doors opened to disclose the dome garden.

This was the nicest place in Ark Three, the circular garden, a kilometre in diameter, protected by a plastic dome, which supplied the fruit and vegetables for the whole underground community. The misters were working and the place smelled fresh and green and wet. Nobody was in sight. Probably the gardeners had gone for lunch while the garden received its daily allotment of water.

She ran along the gravel path that led from the central elevators to the perimeter. By the time she had reached her favourite place, with its view of the eastern mountains, her pale green pant suit was soaked and water was clinging to her curly hair. She shook her head. The wetness didn't matter. The temperature of the garden was kept at twenty-seven degrees Celsius during the day. Her pant suit would soon dry.

The transparent roof joined a waist-high wall around the perimeter, wide enough to sit on. This was Ruth's favourite place, and she scrambled up and sat crosslegged on the top of the wall, leaning against the curved dome.

It's all her fault.

When we're assigned rooms three of us will have to room with her.

It's certainly not going to be me!

Nor me! Nor me! Nor me!

The hateful words echoed round and round in her ears. I'm not going to cry again, she told herself angrily. Crying is babyish and a waste of time.

But what can I do? Life is so completely and absolutely hopeless.

She stared blankly at the distant hills and listed all the things that conspired to make life unbearable.

First of all she was ugly. She was thin and tall, with bony knees and elbows that stuck out and knocked cups off tables and things like that, no matter how hard she tried to concentrate on accidents not happening. Her eyes were slanty and a mixed speckly brown and green, definitely weird. As for her hair, it was a blight. No matter how she tried to be as neat as the rest, her hair would bounce into a wiry tangle.

But it wasn't only looking weird. After all Faith wasn't much to look at, and Purity had a definite squint. It didn't matter because they *meshed.* They were a secure part of the Web, of the whole psychic society that was the community of Ark Three.

And she wasn't. She was not a part of it, not in the least way. Had it always been this bad? She thought back and remembered once earning a gold star in Esper games. That

11

was in Grade One. It was in Grade Six that things had begun to go really wrong.

In Grade Six most people began to show their special Esper skill. It was a difficult time for them all, as they were pulled in two directions, by their newly discovered personal skills and by their communal need to mesh with the whole and be a part of the Web. But she hadn't shown a single useful skill. She couldn't heal; her hands were so clumsy that sick people would probably beg her to go away. She couldn't communicate telepathically with anyone in the City; she couldn't even form the tiny part of the Web that was expected of her without spoiling it. And she most certainly couldn't be a teacher, since she hadn't the least speck of any other skill. All she had were day dreams. Stupid, useless, day dreams.

"What am I to do with my life?" she said out loud. "In four months school will be over and I'll be grown-up. I'm supposed to work for the City, but what can I do? I'll have a room with only three other girls instead of twenty, but no one will share with me. Maybe I'll never have a room. Maybe I'll have to stay in school and dormitory and be a neophyte for ever and ever!"

I think I'd sooner die!

The thought sent a shiver down her spine, because she really couldn't think of an alternative.

As she stared blankly through the transparent plastic of the protecting dome at the wilderness that lay beyond Ark Three, a crazy thought jumped into her mind. Why don't I leave?

It was a terrifying idea. Nobody had ever left the Ark, not since it had been built at the beginning of the Age of Confusion that followed the last of the oil, a hundred and forty years before. That was the purpose of the Ark, to protect the people and their knowledge from the madness that lay outside.

But the madness must be over by now, and nothing seemed to lie outside but meadows and forested foothills and, in the distance, the dark mountains. As Ruth watched, two hawks

12

circled lazily in a thermal, round and round. One of them suddenly plunged to the ground, rising a moment later with a small limp bundle in its talons. There was life outside – animal life anyway – though no signs of human beings. If humans *had* survived the end of civilization outside the Ark, they were somewhere else.

Ruth concentrated on her terrifying thought. If she were to leave the Ark, then the Web would complete itself, golden and shining with psychic energy. She was a flaw in the design. They'd be better off without her. As for the girls in Grade Eight C, they wouldn't have to dread the New Year wondering if she would disgrace them all.

"All right," she said out loud, to make sure she herself believed in her wild plan. "I'll go."

THERE WAS nothing to *stop* a person leaving the Ark, any more than there is anything to stop a person jumping off a ship into a raging sea. It was understood: no one in her right mind would leave the warm togetherness of the Web for the cold empty loneliness of Outside.

The way out was through a door in the western perimeter of Ark Three facing what had been, in the old days, a huge lake, before the dam that had held back the waters had broken. It was on Floor One, where all the foods not grown in the Dome garden, such as yeast cultures and hydroponics, were developed.

The door would be bolted on the inside, of course, since the original purpose of the Ark was to stop the crazies from coming in, not prevent the people of the Ark from leaving. But opening it should be no problem. The problem lay in explaining her presence on Floor One at all. Yeast culture, in particular, was a touchy business and only the scientists actually working were permitted there. In her pale green neophyte's uniform she would stand out, peculiar as usual.

It's hopeless. Completely hopeless. And now I've missed lunch and I'll have to rush back to class or I'll be in trouble again. What were they supposed to be doing this particular afternoon?

Then she remembered and sat up so suddenly that she hit her head against the hard curve of the Dome. She rubbed it absentmindedly, while she busily worked out a plan. That afternoon Eight C was on laundry duty. Everyone from neophyte to Warden took their turn at the jobs necessary to keep the Ark running, from working in the kitchen to shovelling recycled waste for the garden.

If she were to volunteer to sort the laundry it should be easy to borrow a food scientist's white coverall, cap and face mask. As soon as no one was watching she would slip into a washroom, put on the whites and, completely disguised, walk past the yeast vats to the Door.

"I'll do it!" Almost happy again at the thought of action, she ran along the path to the elevators and went downstairs to join her class.

Two hours later she was walking, with as much authority as she could muster, past the yeast culture tanks and vats, towards the western wall. Getting the clothes had been easy. No one ever wanted the job of sorting the smelly overalls used on Floor One. When the sorting was finished, she had carried the bundles to the washing machines and then quietly left.

She looked around her quickly. She mustn't seem unsure of what she was doing, or some officious person would be bound to come up and ask if they could help. Close up her disguise would be useless.

There were half a dozen doors in the western wall, all apparently the doors to storerooms. There seemed to be no Door with a capital D. Well, she would just have to explore and hope she found the right one before someone noticed her.

The first door led to a room lined with shelves filled with dormant cultures. Door number two led to a store of miscellaneous equipment, spare glass vats and tubing. She opened door number three. Her heart was thudding noisily and she

14

could feel the sweat running down her face behind her mask. Surely someone was going to notice her peculiar behaviour.

The room was cluttered with cleaning supplies. Propped against the back wall was a step ladder. She was just about to close the door when she noticed, through the rungs, the outline of another door. A door with great bolts top and bottom!

Ruth slipped into the room and closed the door behind her. Her hands were shaking as she moved the ladder out of the way. If she could open the Door it would be a sign that she was doing the right thing, she told herself, that she was supposed to leave the Ark. She grasped the bottom bolt with both hands. It was stiff with age and wouldn't budge. She wiggled it up and down and pulled again. At last it relented and shot back with a loud *thunk*.

Had anyone heard? She wiped the sweat off her face with rust-stained hands and rubbed her hands down the sides of her pant suit. Then she reached for the top bolt. No good. She had to haul back the ladder and climb up before she could reach it. Had anyone touched the bolts since they were pushed across in the Beginning? She could feel herself trembling, her excitement tearing through the psychic fabric of the Web like shears through synthetic. If she wasn't careful someone would realise what she was doing and catch her before she could get away. She took a deep breath and tried to quieten her unruly mind.

The second bolt slid across. She heaved the ladder out of the way so hastily that it began to topple and she only just grabbed it in the nick of time. Again she stopped and listened, her heart thumping. No one seemed to have heard.

All right, Ruth. Here goes. She turned the door knob and pulled. The hinges creaked and the Door swung open reluctantly. Beyond it, stretching into darkness, was a bare concrete passage.

Not in the dark, she thought. I can't. Her hand fumbled against the inner frame and found a switch. As if by magic the

15

passage sprang into whiteness. She could see straight ahead for about two hundred metres before the line of lights curved out of sight to the left, beckoning her forward to see what lay around the corner.

She shut the Door carefully behind her and took a deep breath. The smell of damp and dust surrounded her. She walked forward, her footsteps echoing loudly. She found herself tiptoeing. What *was* around the corner?

Another hundred metres or so of whitewashed passage ended in a blank wall. Was it all a joke? Was there no way out of the Ark? But that was crazy. No one would build an underground passage going nowhere. Her ancestors *had* to have come through this passage, once the Dome had been sealed over the City. And if the passage led nowhere she would have to go back. To face Patience and Angela and the others . . .

She ran along the last fifty metres, her footsteps echoing loudly. But it was all right. Once she reached the end she could see the ladder set into the lefthand wall. It led up through a round tunnel into darkness above.

She began to climb. Paint flaked off against her hands and rust stained her palms red. How far was it? Not far, she told herself. The Door was only one floor underground. It couldn't be more than three or four metres, could it?

Ouch! She saw stars as her head crashed into something very solid above her. In the faint light from the passage below she saw a round metal cover set in a narrowed collar at the top of the shaft. There was a handle in the centre that had to be pushed around. She slipped one leg through a rung for safety, reached up and pushed.

The handle moved more easily than had the bolts of the door. It swung through a ninety degree arc and the heavy lid fell towards her. She ducked and clung to the ladder as the edge of the heavy lid grazed her shoulder. It swung from its hinges and the noise of its fall echoed up and down the passage.

It died away at last into a silence of dust and ghostly memories and Ruth dared to look up. Above her was more blackness. Another lid!

She forced herself to stand on the topmost rung and reach through the neck to the ladder that logic told her must be there on the other side. Her hands grasped it. She swung through and reached up eagerly to the handle of the second lid.

This one, she worked out, must open outwards. The handle swung easily through its ninety degree arc. She pushed. And pushed again. She climbed a rung higher, so that her shoulder was against it. I won't give up now. Not when I'm so close. She took a deep breath and heaved until her shoulder muscles cracked.

There was a creaking sound. A line of bright light appeared. She pushed again and a blaze of warm sun fell on her face. The lid clanged back and she climbed up blindly into the sunshine and rolled over the edge of the shaft to drop into a bed of sweet-smelling grass.

She was free at last! Free of the Ark and the demands of the Web. She lay on her back in the grass with her eyes still shut, savouring the silence. After a few moments she became aware of a sighing rustle, almost as rhythmic as the air conditioners in the Ark. The wind, she told herself, as it touched her cheek. I am listening to the wind in the grass.

She began to hear other sounds, small creaks and clicks that she couldn't identify. Then, just as had happened in her dream, a sudden buzz made her jump, open her eyes and sit up.

Directly in front of her was the concrete shaft, sticking out of the grass, that was the entrance to Ark Three. Around and beyond it was grass, green and gold, sun-dried, sweet smelling, scattered with flowers. There were grasses with spiked seeds, grasses with plumy purple tops, grasses whose hard heads were speckled with yellow pollen.

She looked down and saw that the small sounds were made by the insects that swarmed everywhere. They were tiny,

17

green-backed, iridescent in the light. They were big, black, lumbering. They were many-jointed, yellow and green, with absurd helmeted heads, that suddenly scared her by jumping a metre at a bound. Some were striped black and yellow, smooth or furry, buzzing furiously as they clung to the flowers.

She could have watched them for hours, but suddenly she remembered where she was and what she had to do. She jumped, unthinkingly, to her feet. No more than two hundred and fifty metres away was the great Dome, its enormous expanse of plastic gleaming silver in the sun. She dropped to her knees in the grass. Had anyone seen her? How stupid it would be to be caught now, after she had been so clever at getting away. Typical Ruth, they would all say.

Cautiously she raised her head above the grass and looked around. To the south the grass stretched in soft curves like a gentle ocean. To the west the river poured into the small lake above the broken dam. To the north and east were the mountains. Her mountains, that had called her ever since . . . ever since when?

She had been twelve when her dreams had begun, she remembered. And in the last year had come the longing for freedom, the need to escape from the Ark and the Web. Into her head drifted a wordless tune. She began to hum it:

Ay-di-doh, ay-di-doh dah-day
Ay-di-doh, ay-di-day-dee . . .

It was an up and going sort of song, and Ruth found herself turning her back on the broken dam and the lake, on the silver eye of the Dome. She strode, as fast as she could, through the shivering grass, towards the east, towards the mountains that piled up, soft green close to, dark behind, with purple mistiness behind that, going on and on for ever.

When she was out of breath she dropped into the grass and lay on her back watching the clouds. Once she was rested she walked on again, her heathery hair bouncing in time to the spritely tune that danced through her head.

18

She must have covered six kilometres or so before the sun slid behind a cloud. At once the mountains ahead of her lost their welcoming glow and looked dour and forbidding. Her legs ached. Her left sandal, which was a little loose, had rubbed a big blister on her heel. She sat down to look at it. It was puffy and the skin around it was red and sore.

Her face burned with the unaccustomed sun and wind. Her lips were cracked and dry. She licked them and thought, how thirsty I am! And then, how hungry!

She groaned and dropped her head onto her knees. "Oh, stupid!" she said aloud. "Now you've done it. Nothing to eat or drink. And no lunch. *Why* didn't I think about food before I left?"

She thought about it now, and she wasn't able to stop thinking about it. Supper. A big juicy soyburger. A tomato. Perhaps even a hard-boiled egg from the chickens that scratched around the Dome garden. And lots of water. Water to drink. To bathe her hot face. To soak her sore feet.

What am I going to do? I won't go back. I can't go back!

As she sat, hunched over the discomfort of her empty stomach, the wind brought her a new message. In fact she had been hearing it for some time without understanding it. It was the sound of running water. Over there. To the left.

She took off her ill-fitting sandals and walked barefoot through the grass. The sound grew clearer and closer. The long grass became short. The short grass turned to moss. And there it was, right at her feet. A small stony brook, too small to be on any map, trickling down the hillside.

She fell on her stomach and splashed her hot face and drank. The water was surprisingly cold for August. She drank until her stomach no longer felt empty. Then she sat on a lichen-painted stone and soaked her sore feet until they turned numb and white and she could not feel the pain in her heel.

Feeling better, she fastened her sandals as securely as she could and got to her feet. How stiff she was. Her calves ached. Her thighs ached. But she had hardly walked any distance at

19

all. She could still see Ark Three, the dome an almost perfect circle on the meadowland to the north-west far below her.

She plodded uphill, trying to ignore the ache in her legs and the throbbing pain that returned to her heel as soon as the numbness wore off. At last, when the sun had dropped below the smoky purple line of the western hills, she began to look for a place to sleep.

Trees grew on the slope above her, and among them Ruth felt more comfortable. She curled up at the foot of one giant, on a bed of fallen and decayed leaves. She dozed and woke, stiff-necked and cold.

The stars were out. How different they looked here from the warm security of the Dome. There, they had been a familiar pattern that defined time and season, as if the Ark itself were a cog in the works of some enormous clock.

Here they were individuals, burning down on her, hard and unwinking, as if to say: What are you doing out here, you troublesome human? Go back underground where your kind belong. Leave the Earth you tried to destroy to heal its wounds in peace.

But it wasn't me, she thought, feeling like an interfering grain of sand in the works. All that happened years and years before I was born. Now we understand about peace and friendship, and about respect for nature and for each other. That's what the Ark is all about.

Then what are you doing here? the stars accused. If the Ark is all peace and friendship why did you run away? Go back.

"I can't," Ruth wailed out loud. She shivered at the loneliness of her voice in the still, unfriendly night. "I can't. I don't belong there."

But you don't belong here either, the cold stars seemed to say. Ruth crumpled onto the ground and wept for loneliness and hopelessness.

The next thing she knew, she was in the middle of one of her dreams. She was inside the body and the feelings of a boy, which was a strange and uncomfortable place to be.

20

Somehow she knew that he was the same boy she had dreamed about often before. Only this dream was clearer, clearer than any of them had been before.

She – or rather he – was standing beside a river, reaching out his hands towards a girl, clothed in a simple tunic of fur, whose red hair flowed untrimmed down her brown back. The boy was saying goodbye, but she would not answer. She turned away, her face like stone, and in the end he splashed across the river away from her.

Ruth felt his pain as if it were her own. He was leaving happiness and freedom, going to something he detested and dreaded. She tried to struggle with the dream body, to force him to turn back, to cross the river again, to run after the red-haired girl before it was too late.

"I have to go . . ." he muttered, and another man ahead of him on the trail turned and said, "What's that?"

Ruth woke with a jolt, the moon full on her face. She felt cold, and lonely with a loneliness that was not hers alone. On the slopes below were lights and she could hear voices. For a moment her dream self welcomed them as friends. Then she remembered and staggered to her feet. She was Ruth. There was no one in the wilderness but herself. Had the people from the Ark found her? She turned and began to run.

2
The Dream closes in

"STOP!" The command thundered in her head and Ruth stumbled and fell to the ground. Running feet crunched the dead leaves. Then she was picked up and brushed down with gentle hands. "There now. There."

It was one of the Healers, Ruth couldn't see which in the shadows that danced around their torches. The rest of the group who crowded around were all in the blue uniform of Communicators, and with them . . . her heart missed a beat . . . was the Warden himself.

"Let me go, please. It's no good."

"What is no good?" The Warden must be very angry, she thought, though his voice sounded kind enough.

"Me. I can't mesh with the others. They hate me. I'll never be a proper part of the Web and I'm just spoiling it for everyone else."

"Never is a very harsh word. Who told you that you'd never be part of the Web?"

"No one. I just know it, that's all."

"And you expect us to turn our backs on one of our precious members and just let you go – like that?"

Ruth didn't feel like a precious member of anything, and wondered if it was just the Warden's grand way of talking. She nodded dumbly.

"And what will you do out here in the wasteland?"

"I'll . . . I'll be . . . " How could she describe freedom? The lilting song that had helped her feet across the meadowland

and up the hill came into her mind and she found she was singing it. This time it had words.

> "I'll be free to think and free to grow
> Under a sky so blue,
> Down in the fields where the flowers blow,
> Part of a world made new."

What was she saying? Where had the words come from? Her hands went to her face. "I'm going crazy. I know I am." She began to cry.

"Hush. It's all right." The Warden's voice was full of authority, but Ruth couldn't stop crying. The yellow-uniformed Healer put her hands on her head.

A warmth began to spread through Ruth's body. She felt numb and her eyes slid shut. "No," she whispered. "Don't make me."

SHE WOKE with the feeling that she had overslept, after hours of dreaming a crazy dream about Outside. She opened her eyes and stared. This wasn't the familiar dormitory. She was in a small yellow-painted room, alone. In the hospital then. So it *had* happened. She closed her eyes tightly and wished she was outside again, among the grass and the flowers, with the sun hot on her head and shoulders. She didn't let herself remember the dark and the cold and the loneliness. Oh, if only they'd let her be...

Healer Mercy Smith came into the room with a tray. "Good, you're awake at last. Here's breakfast – or maybe we'd better call it lunch!"

Ruth sat up. "How did you know where I'd gone?"

"It wasn't too difficult, my dear. Once you were missed in your group the Communicators checked through the Ark. They found the Door unbolted. How very enterprising of you!"

"I suppose I shall get into the most awful trouble."

23

"You were rather a nuisance, you know. But I wouldn't worry. Eat up."

"But how did you find me outside? There is so much . . . so much space."

Mercy laughed. "Do you think you're immune from Esper thought? You left a trail as clear as sign posts. Now eat up. You must be starving."

"But . . ."

"Later."

Ruth discovered that she *was* starving. Outside was wonderful, but it would be impossible to survive without food. Perhaps it was a good thing after all that her Esper trail had been so clear. But it was odd. She had thought . . . after all, she was so bad at meshing . . . Then she stopped worrying and cleaned up her plate.

Two hours later, showered, changed into clean uniform and checked out as perfectly healthy in spite of her escapade, Ruth reluctantly pushed open the door of the Grade Eight C classroom and slid into her desk, wishing that she could just be invisible. Angela was bound to mock her in her odious way, and all the others would laugh.

Maths passed somehow, and then History. The bell rang for lunchtime and she hunched her shoulders against the expected barbs of Angela's tongue.

"Come on, Ruth," Angela ordered. "You're to sit next to me at lunch."

"Not fair, Angie. I bagged her first."

"And what about us?"

"Huh?" Ruth stared. No-one had ever fought over who should sit next to her. That honour was reserved for the golden girls: the Angelas, the Patiences . . .

"Oh, come on." Angela linked her arm through Ruth's. "We'll get tidied up and work out the seating on the way to the dining room."

In a dream Ruth washed her hands and tried to smooth down her wiry hair. She allowed herself to be escorted to the dining room, where Faith ran ahead to bag a table on the girls' side.

"Now you sit here. Don't stir. Faith will bring your tray."

Maybe I'm going to be popular after all, thought Ruth. Maybe it's something that suddenly happens to you, like getting your second teeth or becoming a woman. I was just later than the others.

"Now tell us *all* about it," Angela demanded, when they were all seated with their lunches. Ruth looked at her. There was no friendship in her eyes, only avid curiosity.

"About . . . ?" She played for time.

"Oh, don't be dense! What it was like Outside, of course. I must say, I didn't think you had the nerve."

Ruth put her spoon down reluctantly. It would be hard to share her experience, even with a best friend. But she had to say something. They were all waiting, all staring at her. "It smelt so fresh. That was the first thing I noticed. And the wind was cool even though the sun was hot. It . . ." She stopped.

"Well, go on."

"It was free. Quiet and free."

"Sounds totally boring." Angela shrugged. The others echoed her judgment. Boring.

"I want to know why you did it," whispered Honesty.

"Well . . . " Ruth looked at their faces. Their eyes were like the bars of a cage. She could not escape. "It's just too hard to explain."

"Someone said that you were crazy about one of the boys in Eight, but he wasn't interested because you're so . . . well, you know."

"Is that it, Ruth?" Angela's voice was like a knife. "Who is it? Benedict? Or maybe Justin?"

A shiver of excitement ran around the table. If the Warden should catch them talking about *boys*! Why, boys were not supposed to exist until the New Year and Graduation.

"That's ridiculous." Ruth's voice went up indignantly.

25

"Hush. Do you want to get us into trouble, you stupid thing?"

"Well, it *is* ridiculous. We never even get to meet boys until next year. How could I possibly be in love with one of them?"

Charity giggled. "What a child you are! We see them in the library and at meal-times, don't we?" She leaned across the table. "See the tall one with the black hair and the eyebrows that go straight across? Fidelius. Bet you I get to meet him before the New Year. Bet you I *talk* to him in next library period."

As the girls giggled together Ruth was, for the moment, forgotten and could finish her dinner in peace. It wasn't until they were on their way back to their classroom that Charity opened the attack again. "I know you're in love with someone, so you can just stop pretending."

"I'm not. What a story!" Ruth found herself blushing.

"It isn't then. I've heard you call out his name in your sleep."

"Who is it? Tell us," the others teased, but Ruth shook her head angrily.

"It's something like Browan," Charity disclosed. "Don't deny it, you sly thing. I've heard you ... Browan ... Browan." Her wail sent the rest into giggles.

"There isn't ... it isn't ... " Ruth ran ahead of her tormentors into the classroom.

The afternoon dragged on. At least I missed Web Practice today, Ruth consoled herself. But there's still the Warden to face.

The summons came in the middle of dish drying after supper. "Ruth, go to the Warden's office."

There was silence as she hung her cloth carefully on the line and walked across the big kitchen. Only when she had crossed the threshold did the voices break out behind her, Charity's clear above the babble. "After what she did I bet they put her in the Hole."

Ruth flinched and clenched her hands into fists. The Black Hole. The ultimate punishment on Ark Three. In fact the *only* punishment. Just the name was enough to send a shiver down the spine of the naughtiest neophyte in Junior School. The Black Hole.

In fact Ruth knew very little about it, or even where it was. But it was there. And after you had been in it an hour, or a day – rumours varied – you came out shattered and repentant.

But I didn't really do anything wrong, Ruth told herself as she made her trembling way along to the Warden's office.

She said as much to him after he had made her sit beside him on the sofa. "I really didn't mean to do anything wrong. I wanted to leave because I was spoiling the Web for everyone else. The girls all despise me, and there didn't seem to be anything to do *except* run away."

"Now just a minute. What do you mean, spoiling the Web?"

She tried to explain her distractions and daydreams.

"Like this, you mean?" He showed her a reading off a psychic potentiometer.

She blushed. "Yes. See that jagged line. That was me. I'm no good and I'll never be an Esper no matter how hard I try. So if I can't be part of the Web what's the use of staying?"

"I could say: What's the point of going? You know you couldn't survive out there alone. But why did you say you'll never be an Esper? Where did you get that curious idea?"

"Look at that psi trace, Warden. My score pulled down the class average. Angela said there had never been one so low. She . . ."

The Warden put a hand over Ruth's. It was warm and comforting. She looked up in surprise to meet grey eyes that were full of kindness. "You're going to have to believe me when I tell you that you have a very powerful Esper gift. You couldn't have made that trace with nothing. The only problem is that your power is not going in the same direction as most other people's. It's as if a team of horses were pulling a

27

load – you do know what horses are, don't you? – and an elephant was harnessed to pull the load in the other direction. Can you imagine what would happen?"

"They'd cancel each other out. And that's what's happening to the Grade Eight Web. And it's just as bad, isn't it? Since I'm not a Healer or a Communicator or a Teacher or anything useful it would be better for the Great Pattern if you were to let me leave." She blinked back angry tears.

"Oh my word, what have we been teaching you?" The Warden sprang to his feet and began to walk up and down his office in such an agitated way that Ruth wondered what on earth she had said. He stopped in front of her. "Listen to me, Ruth. The whole purpose of the Ark is to develop a strong people dedicated to peace, justice and loving kindness to their fellow humans. Right?"

She nodded.

"Well, thank goodness! I began to wonder." He smiled down at her and then went on seriously. "Our chief tool has been Extrasensory Perception. The Ark was deliberately populated with a high Esper population. We have been working to strengthen the Web ever since – to complete the Great Pattern in which humankind's virtues will work so strongly that they can overcome the weaknesses of greed, avarice, anger, envy, all the faults that led to the Age of Confusion. Do you understand?"

"Yes, of course, Warden. I've studied City History for *eight* years."

"My apologies. I had forgotten how nearly grown up you were."

She shot a suspicious glance at him. Was he laughing at her? His mouth was serious, but his grey eyes twinkled. He went on. "Knowing our history and what we are trying to achieve, can you not see that to throw away a precious human being, to discard someone just because she does not fit the pattern, would be to deny everything that we say we believe in?"

28

"But if I *choose* to go," she said at last. "Then it wouldn't be your fault, would it?"

He shook his head. "That argument won't work. If we had made you so unhappy that life here wasn't worth living, that it made more sense to you to walk out into the wilderness . . ."

"Then what am I going to *do*? It's all so hopeless."

"It's never hopeless. Don't even think that. Go on with your growing up. We'll help you all we can. I'll speak to Teacher Jonson. Perhaps your class mates . . . ?"

"Oh no. Please not." To be known as the Warden's pet would be worse than anything.

"Very well. Off you go, my dear. It must be past your bedtime."

"Then . . . you're not going to send me to the Hole?"

"The . . . ? Oh, gracious me, no. Whatever put that idea into your head. Off you go and stop worrying so much about yourself."

WHICH WAS easy enough to say, thought Ruth, lying in the Grade Eight C dormitory, listening to the sleepers' breathing and the soft whisper of the air conditioner. She fell asleep at last and dreamed the clearest dream she had ever had. When she woke at the bell it was to a sense that the dormitory, the showers, the crowded dining room were all much less real than the world of her dream.

During art class they were supposed to paint a subconscious impression of their relationship to the Web. Dreamily Ruth mixed green paints and washed in on her paper the impression of a field, with trees in the background of a darker colour, smoky and mysterious. Between the trees slanted sunlight, gold, dusty. That was almost impossible to get right. She painted on, her tongue between her teeth.

In the foreground of the picture was a girl with arms and legs brown instead of pinky white, wearing a short tunic instead of a pant suit. What was it made of? Something rough

29

and soft at the same time, shaped rather than woven. In the girl's hands was a long stick with a metal piece at one end. She was leaning forward in the picture, so that her red hair fell about her shoulders, hiding her face.

"Time, girls. Bring up your paintings and pin them on the board."

Ruth painted on, humming under her breath. She had found a way to paint the hairiness in the tunic, using an almost dry brush.

"Ruth!"

She jumped, looked up and saw everyone standing at the front of the room. "Yes, Teacher Jonson?"

"Your drawing, please."

"Oh, yes." She snatched the wet paper, fell over the desk and scurried to the front.

"Pin it up with the others, then." Teacher Jonson turned to look at the other work. "Patience, will you explain the significance of the colours you have chosen?"

The lesson went on. Ruth stared at her painting. What had she done? It was her dream exactly. But how could she possibly explain it?

Teacher Jonson turned, looked at Ruth's drawing for a long moment and then removed it from the board. "No giggling, please, girls. Pay attention."

She didn't say one word to Ruth, and at the end of the class Ruth escaped from the comments of the others and went up to the Dome. What was there beyond the eastern mountains that drew her as iron filings are drawn to a magnet? That was where her dream had come from, and somewhere beyond that range of hills was something without which she would never be whole.

But they'll never let me leave. I'll have to stay for ever, never being a part of the Web. I wish I were old. I wish my life was practically over. No, I don't mean that. Not yet. Not till I've had a chance to live and be myself. If only they'll let me.

30

RUTH went to bed thinking about escape, and that night the nightmare came. She was falling down a wellshaft, falling and falling for a very long time. Then she was in icy water, choking, fighting to get free. She woke in terror, with the sheets tangled around her legs. Her mouth was dry and her throat ached as if she had been screaming.

"What's going on?"

"Is it a fire?"

She tried to shrink down under the tangled bedclothes, but at that moment the light was snapped on. There was Angela, frowning like an avenging angel.

"Ruth? Well, I suppose I should have guessed. What are you doing, screaming like that?"

"I didn't mean to, honestly, Angela. I'm sorry I woke you. It was just a . . . a dream," she finished feebly, looking at the sleepy hostile faces. She lay down and shut her eyes tightly. The light clicked off. As soon as the room was quiet once more she sat up, her hands clasped round her knees. I won't go back to sleep, she vowed. Not to *that*.

She fell asleep the next night as soon as her head touched the pillow. And the dream was back. There was the same sense of falling, of being trapped in a place from which there was no escape. Then there was ice cold water in her mouth and nose. She fought to keep her head up for what felt like hours, and woke, tangled in bedclothes, with Angela standing over her.

"Two nights in a row! That does it. I'm going to tell a Healer so we can get some sleep around here."

"Please, Angela, don't make a fuss. I'm fine. I won't wake you up again, honest I won't."

"Will you come with me, or do I have to fetch a Healer here?"

"I'll come. I'll come." Ruth hunted under her bed for her slippers. She couldn't find them anywhere. Her dressing gown was halfway down the room, as if someone had thrown it, and she tripped over her pillow on the way to the door.

"Oh, come *on*."

"I am. I can't find my slippers."

Angela grabbed her arm and dragged her through the door.

"Ouch, ouch!"

"What's the matter now?"

"Stubbed my toe."

Angela sighed. "Ruth, you are a mess. When are you going to get yourself together? In less than five months it's going to be New Year. Look at your clothes, at your bed. No wonder you can't find anything."

"I didn't make that mess, honestly. It was perfectly tidy when I went to bed. And you're hurting!" She pulled her arm away and walked along the corridor ahead of Angela.

THE Healer was very kind. Of course they were always kind. "You'd better spend the rest of the night in a cubicle here."

Ruth drew back. "I'd rather not go to sleep again. Couldn't I just sit up and read a book?"

"It was that bad, eh? Why don't you tell me about it?"

But when Ruth had described the nightmare all the Healer said was, "Why, that's quite a common dream. I expect it's just a remnant of your birth memory surfacing from your subconscious ..."

"But it was terrifying. I thought I was going to die. Being born is beautiful, isn't it?"

"Of course. But in spite of music and soft light and everyone's comforting thoughts it is still a scary event in a baby's life, being pushed out of a comfortable womb into the cold world. In just a few months you'll be entering the adult world of Ark Three. Are you scared about that? Maybe part of you wants to remain a comfortable neophyte."

Ruth felt like telling the Healer just how miserable it was to be a neophyte, if you were a person who didn't fit in; but it seemed impolite to contradict, so she said nothing.

The Healer patted her shoulder. "Have a good night's sleep. If the dream comes back remind yourself that being born is a great and exciting adventure, nothing to be afraid of."

Alone in the cubicle, a little comforted, though not entirely convinced, for the dream had felt so real, Ruth lay down and obediently shut her eyes.

Then the dream was back: the falling, the icy water, the sense of suffocation. She was aware, for the first time, of the noise. It was all about her, the roar of water, echoing, crashing.

"It is the dream of being born," she told herself as she struggled. "And being born is a great and . . . " She woke with a jolt and a scream to find herself sitting up in bed. The sheets and pillows were on the floor and the little night table had been overturned.

The Healer came running in. "Did I hear you call? It's all right. Nothing to worry about. Just a little earth tremor, I expect. Enough to scare anyone."

"A tremor?"

"Just enough to pop all the cupboard doors open. And knock over your night table, I see." She picked it up. "The bulb in your lamp is broken. You won't be needing it, will you? I must get back and clean up the broken glass. You wouldn't believe what rolled out of the cupboards. Goodnight."

She bustled off. For the remainder of the night Ruth lay staring at the dark ceiling and pinching her arm whenever she felt her eyes close. She longed for the lights to come on, for the night to end.

Outside, she thought, the lights won't come on to wake you up or go out when it's time for sleep. You would have to wake and sleep with the sun. How strange that would be. She lay and thought about the golden sun until it was time to get up.

After two broken nights she was quite light-headed during class. The melody that had fallen into her mind when she was Outside kept surfacing until, in dance class, in the middle of a formal set that was supposed to illustrate the Oneness of the Web, the melody took her over.

> "So the Freedom Man danced out of the Ark
> Over the hills so shady,
> Into the light and out of the dark
> With his long-haired lady . . . "

She hummed happily and let the tune spin her round and round until she was dizzy.

"Ruth, stop that at once."

She stopped. She'd done it again. Nineteen pairs of eyes accused her. Her cheeks hot, she slipped into her place between Angela and Charity. Angela pinched the back of her hand.

"Show off!"

"Ouch!"

"What was that?" The dance teacher spun around. Angela looked blandly innocent. Ruth put her smarting hand behind her back. "Ruth, are you quite ready?"

"Yes, Teacher Forman."

"Very well. Girls, begin again."

Class dragged on. Ruth was thankful when they were dismissed for library period. The other girls pushed past her as if she didn't exist and hurried down the corridor. Library period was popular, as there was always a chance of seeing, sometimes even of exchanging a surreptitious word with one of the boys.

Charity brashly skipped over to a shelf where the tall dark boy she had pointed out the other day in the dining hall was standing. Half amused, Ruth watched Charity's technique as she skimmed along the shelf, picking up a book, reading a couple of lines, putting it back and picking up another until, so casually that you would have sworn it was by chance, she reached out at the exact moment and to the exact place where Fidelius was putting his book back in the shelf. Their hands touched. They smiled. Ruth could see by the movement of their lips that they were whispering.

Then Teacher Jonson swooped down and Charity was sent with the book she still had in her hand to sit in the farthest corner of the library.

And I hope it's something too boring for words, thought Ruth. Silly idiot!

She went over to the fiction section and picked out an adventure story from the long ago days. It was called *Lorna Doone*, and she had already read several chapters. Now she lost herself in the adventures of the hero, John Ridd, as he climbed the cliff to find himself in the forbidden Doone Valley.

Like my dream country, she thought. Somewhere beyond the eastern mountains is a valley. And in the valley . . . well, what?

She stared at the windowless walls and longed to be up in the Dome where she could see out.

"The Freedom Man danced out of the Ark
Over the hills so shady,
Into the light and out of the dark
To be with his red-haired lady."

The tune danced maddeningly in her head. Where had it come from? Who was the Freedom Man? Someone like John Ridd? And was the red-haired lady the same person as the one she had painted? It was all very strange. She sighed and went on reading until suppertime.

That night there was no nightmare, but the trouble surfaced again in art class the next day. Teacher Jonson had put a cassette of soft music into the player. They had done their breathing exercises, lying in a circle on the floor, their hands lightly touching.

"Now get up slowly and go to your places. Paint your impression of the Web. Stay relaxed. Don't let your logical mind take over. Stay with your meditation images."

I will draw the Web, Ruth told herself severely, as she took up her brush. I will *not* draw my dreams. I *will* draw the Web...

She washed grey over her paper and slashed it with a tracery of fine black lines. In the centre was a figure. With her tongue between her teeth she concentrated on getting it right.

"Time, everyone. Don't worry if you're not finished. First impressions are what count in this exercise. Pin them up and we'll discuss your different ideas."

Ruth hurried to stick her picture up in a corner of the board, and turned her attention to Faith's painting. It was a series of concentric rings with a glow of gold in the middle, most beautiful. Patience had painted a mosaic of pinks, mauves and blues. Charity's was very self-conscious. She's still thinking about Fidelius, Ruth guessed.

She became aware that the others had crowded over to the far end of the board. That they were nudging each other. Giggling. Staring at *her*. What had she done this time?

There it was. A spider's web, with a revoltingly fat and hairy spider crouched in the middle. To make bad much much worse, the spider had four heads, each one an obvious caricature of the Protector, the Custodian, the Initiator and the Warden of the City! Had she really painted that grotesque thing?

She tried to grab it, but Teacher Jonson's hand was ahead of hers. The painting was whisked away into a folder, the folder into a drawer.

"Oh, please. I didn't mean ... "

"That's quite enough, Ruth."

"You can't show them. You simply can't. I'll ... I'll ... "

There was a sudden racket of doors banging up and down the corridor.

"Yes?" said Teacher Jonson, eyeing Ruth sternly.

"Nothing." Ruth collapsed at her desk.

"Dinnertime. Go and get tidy."

Ruth followed the others out of the door.

"What got into you?" hissed Angela as they lined up for their food.

"I don't want to talk about it."

"You don't want to . . . Do you know what you're doing to our reputation? What is New Year's Day going to be like with a crazy like you in the class."

"Angela, don't . . . "

Angela was looking over her shoulder at Ruth. She didn't see the bowl of tomatoes tip off the service counter right in front of her. The tomatoes cascaded to the floor.

"Aaaah!" Angela skidded in the juicy fruit.

"Watch out!" Ruth tried to grab her.

Flat on her back, her tray scattered, tomatoes staining her hair and uniform, Angela glared up at Ruth. "You pushed me! You deliberately pushed me. I'm going to report you to the Warden."

"She didn't touch you, Angela." Patience hauled the furious Angela to her feet. "It was just an accident."

Angela will never believe that, thought Ruth. I think if the roof fell in she'd blame me for it. Maybe it *is* my fault. I really wanted something horrible to happen to her. She picked at her lunch and left most of it uneaten.

The day dragged on. She broke two dishes on kitchen duty, just because her hands were shaking so. It was almost a relief when the summons finally came.

"Ruth, go to the Warden's office."

"Skipping dishes is getting to be a habit," Faith joked quite kindly.

Ruth smiled weakly and scurried down the corridor to the Warden's office. She knocked very softly. Maybe he won't hear. Maybe he's been called away.

"Come in."

She pushed the door open and drew back. Oh, no! Not just the Warden, but all four of them, the Custodian, the Protector and the Initiator as well.

They were all seated on the far side of the Warden's desk,

with the evidence of her crimes in front of them. From the door she could see the painting of a red-haired girl, a pile of her essays and stories, and that awful, insulting picture of the Web.

"Sit down over here, dear child."

Ruth managed to creep across the room and collapse into the chair the Protector had indicated. She wound both her legs out of the way around the legs of the chair. Then she twined her fingers together in her lap and stared at them.

"It's really very clever," said the Protector, so unexpectedly that she looked up and saw him holding the Web painting. "Do you really see us like that?"

"I don't know, Protector. I suppose I must. But I didn't mean . . . " Her voice trailed off.

In the silence the Custodian took over. "My dear, we have spent some time going over your drawings and essays – in fact all your responses to class situations for the last few years, and we are very puzzled. It is almost as if you were living in a different world."

Ruth's mouth opened. How did they know? The Custodian waited for her to speak, and then went on. "Let's look at this drawing of the girl with red hair. It is most imaginative, but rather confusing. For instance, do you know what she's holding in her hand?"

"It's a kind of pole, Custodian."

"But what is it for? Do you know what the girl is supposed to be doing?"

"She's doing something to the plants down there." Ruth was less scared now. They seemed to be interested rather than angry. "That triangle at the end is supposed to be sharp. I think she's kind of stirring up the soil around the plants."

"I see. Well, that makes sense. Now about her clothing – you seem to have had some difficulty in deciding what she was supposed to be wearing."

"Oh, no." She spoke eagerly. "I know exactly what it's supposed to look like. It's just so difficult to paint right. It's soft and hairy, not a bit like synthetic cloth."

"Fur perhaps, like the skin of an animal." The Initiator touched the surface of the paper with one finger.

"Yes, that's right. How clever of you to know." She stopped and blushed at her temerity.

"But the point is that you're not making up these drawings, are you?" The Warden fixed her with a rather severe look. "You're trying to put down something that is very clear to you – something you remember. Is that right?"

"Yes, Warden. That's what we're supposed to do in art class. Put down just what's in our head."

"In *your* head."

"Yes, Warden."

There was another silence. Then the Custodian reached over and lifted a fat folder off the desk. Is that all about *me*? thought Ruth guiltily, and slouched down into her chair.

"Now where is that report I'm looking for? Ah, here it is. When Ruth was picked up outside the Dome."

Ruth blushed and sank even lower in her chair.

"Let me see. . . The Warden said 'If we let you go what would you do, Ruth?' Do you remember what you replied, Ruth?"

"N...no. No, I don't think I do."

"You sang a song. Do you remember the words? Do you, Ruth?"

"Yes, Custodian."

"Could you sing it for us now?"

Ruth shook her head and stared at the floor.

"You sang the following strange words:

> 'The Freedom Man danced out of the Ark
> Over the hills so shady
> Into the light and out of the dark
> With his long-haired lady.'

Do you remember that?"

"Yes, ma'am."

"And the tune. Do you recollect the tune?"

"Of course I do. It's in my head all the time. It's driving me crazy!" Ruth's fingers stretched out and her legs unwound from around the chair legs. At the same instant the papers on the desk flew up into the air, funnelled up to the ceiling and then drifted down again. "Oh, what's happened!"

The Protector jumped to his feet and ran around the desk to stand behind Ruth, his hands resting lightly on her shoulders. "It's all right, Ruth. Steady. Nobody's going to hurt you."

"How did that . . . it can't be another earth tremor, can it? I didn't feel anything. And then there were the tomatoes. They just flew off the counter. Oh, I'm scared!"

The papers fluttered again and the Custodian spread her hands over them. "Now listen, Ruth," she said. "And for goodness' sake keep calm. There can be two answers to what is happening to you. Either the song and the paintings, all the rest, have come out of your imagination because you're not having a very happy time growing up and they form a kind of escape world for you." Ruth shook her head. The papers fluttered. "Or," the Custodian continued firmly, "there actually exists, outside the Ark, a place of which you are dreaming and drawing, with which you are, in some strange way, in contact."

"And you believe it could be real?" Ruth looked up in sudden hope.

"Yes."

"How can you find out?"

There was a silence, broken at last by the Protector. "Friends, I know of only one way of discerning whether these events are real and objective, received through the Esper faculties of Ruth. Or if they are only in her imagination." He paused and Ruth could feel his fingers suddenly hard, biting into the muscles of her shoulders.

"Yes, Protector?" The other three looked at him.

"Ruth must be put into the Black Hole!"

40

3
The Black Hole

RUTH SCREAMED and struggled. Books flew across the Warden's office and slammed into the opposite wall. The Protector's fingers still gripped her shoulders. She felt his psychic strength fight hers and for a moment she exulted in the knowledge that she was stronger than he, that she was winning. But then the energy seemed to drain from her body and she slumped forward.

When she opened her eyes the first thing she was aware of was blackness. She was lying on her back staring up at a black ceiling. She turned her head reluctantly, afraid of what she might see. But there was no doubt. Four black walls surrounded her. She raised her head and looked down. The floor was also black.

Obviously the room was lit, but it was so cunningly done that she could not see where the light was coming from. Her throat tightened. The Protector had carried out his threat and put her in the Black Hole. The ultimate punishment on Ark Three. Fragments of stories floated into her mind. "... and when they let him out his hair had turned completely white." "... she was there for less than an hour, but when they unlocked the door she was a gibbering idiot!"

Ruth sat up and hugged her knees to her chest, waiting for the horror, whatever it was, to begin. Nothing happened. She listened to the thudding of her heart, which was the only sound, and told herself: I won't let them see that I'm afraid. Whatever it is. Whatever they do. I just won't!

41

The memory of an ancient story she had read in the library jumped into her mind. What was it called? *The Pit and the Pendulum*, that was it. The hero had been a prisoner in a place of horror, rather like this. And then . . . She stared up at the ceiling, imagining that at any moment a knife blade would come swinging down, slicing through the air, to and fro, lower and lower. In spite of herself she shrank back onto the couch, making herself as flat as possible .

But of course nothing like that really happened. Nothing happened at all, and after a time she just lay on her back staring up at the blackness. It was most extraordinary, this black room. It was hard to define its edges, to guess how high the ceiling must be, how far away the walls.

After a time she began to feel that she was floating weightlessly in the black void of space. Briefly she remembered the second part of Poe's story, in which the floor opened up and the walls moved inward so that he would either be crushed or hurled into a fiery abyss far below. "But it's only a story," she said out loud, no longer afraid. Her words were absorbed by the blackness around her. She had never felt such quiet, such peace. Her eyes shut and she slept.

SHE WOKE feeling that she had slept deeply, better than she had done in months. She sat up and swung her legs down from the couch. What was so different? Why did she feel newly made?

Why, of course! There had been no dreams, not a single one. The silence she felt around her was more than the silence of an empty room. It was a room from which all the psychic clutter, that was part of everyday life on Ark Three, had been removed. She could feel her mind stretching out without bumping against the mind of another person. It was a room without the Web.

She lay down again, better to enjoy the peace. She was still resting, her hands behind her head, when she heard the sound of a latch. She turned her head lazily to see who it was.

An oblong of light shone upon one wall. Space established itself once more in her little domain. The walls rushed in and the ceiling seemed to descend, not as in Poe's story, but to show her that the reality of the Black Hole was not illimitable space, but a little room not much larger than a closet.

She recognised the tall figure silhouetted against the golden light of the passage outside. It was the Initiator. Ruth slid off the couch and stood politely waiting as she entered the room and shut the door behind her. At once the illusion of space returned and the prickly agitation, that she had begun to feel through the open door, vanished.

"How do you feel?" The Initiator smiled.

"Wonderful. Relaxed and free. And I slept – oh, how I slept. Without a single dream."

"I know."

"How could you possibly . . .?" Ruth stopped and blushed at her rudeness.

The Initiator laughed and motioned her to sit beside her on the couch. "It was easy. No more slammed doors. No more broken glass."

"That really *was* me? I did that with my mind?"

"You certainly did. Oh, don't worry about it. You're not to blame. We should have diagnosed you far sooner."

"Diagnosed? Do you mean I'm sick or something?"

"Far from it. Ruth, do you know what psychokinesis is?"

"I think so. Isn't it the movement of physical objects by the use of the mind alone?"

"That's right. And we have finally realised that you are a powerful, though completely uncontrolled, psychokinetic. You're only the second PK to turn up in a generation, which is why we didn't catch you sooner."

"Well, thank goodness the Black Hole cured me. I feel wonderful – as light as air. But it's funny. I thought . . ." She stopped.

"What's the problem?"

"I thought the Black Hole was supposed to be a terrible punishment."

The Initiator laughed. "The things that neophytes dream up! Did you think you'd come out stark mad or with your hair turned white? I remember those stories going around when I was in Grade Eight. But of course we had no intention of punishing you. Only of making sure of our diagnosis. Ruth, do you know what insulation is?"

"A non-conductor. Something that stops the passage of heat or electricity."

"That and more. It is also used to dampen out sound waves – or in this case psychic noise. The Black Hole is nothing more than a room designed to insulate out the psychic emanations of the Ark and vice versa."

Ruth tried to look intelligent. The Initiator laughed. "Suppose there was a noisy party going on and you wanted to go to sleep, it wouldn't be a problem if you had a sound-proofed sleeping cubicle, would it?"

"Oh, I do see. The psychic noise of everyone in the Ark was bothering me so much that I couldn't sleep properly and that's why I had all those crazy dreams and got irritable and . . . and so on."

"Well, it's a little more complicated than that, but more or less."

"I don't understand why the Web doesn't bother anyone else?"

"That's a bit harder to explain. Imagine a group of musicians playing together. If their instruments are tuned to each other and they play well you will get a harmonious sound. But if there is an instrument that's made differently, that cannot be precisely tuned to the others, then you get discord."

"That's exactly the way I felt when the girls were talking about me spoiling everything. I thought what a shame it was for me to ruin the sound of the whole orchestra. That's why I ran away. You should have let me go, Initiator."

"We've been through that before, Ruth. You are a human

being, as precious as every other person in Ark Three. You have your own part to play in the making of the Great Design, perhaps a little part, perhaps very important – who knows? We just have to work harder to find out what it is."

"Well, I certainly can't imagine." Ruth sighed.

"Cheer up and stop feeling so sorry for yourself. Listen, Ruth. We had two reasons for leaving you overnight in the Black Hole. We wanted to prove that it was your PK psyche that was the cause of the little disturbances we've been having. Not earth tremors." Her lips twitched into a smile. "We also had to make sure that the dreams, the drawings, the songs, were based on some messages from the real world outside the Ark, and not on some imagined schizophrenic world."

"You mean mad, don't you? What did you find out?"

"Bless you, child. You're as normal as the rest of us."

"Are you sure? Absolutely sure?"

"Ruth, if your dreams were the product of your own disturbed mind, why wouldn't they continue in here? You brought your whole mind with you."

"I don't think I ..."

"If you had developed an imaginary world so real that you dreamed about it, sang songs about it, drew it, thought about it constantly, do you think you would have been able to leave it outside the Black Hole, just like that?"

"Suppose it's the psychic noise of the Web crowding me that brings on the dreams?"

"We don't believe you would have made such a spectacular recovery."

"So it *is* real. I was sure it was, you know. That was the scariest part. I mean, that's what you'd think if you *were* going crazy, wouldn't you? But what is it? What am I receiving?"

"Messages from another psychic community."

"Out there? Human beings?"

"So we believe. Oh, you have a rare and tremendous gift. But you're untrained. The messages are garbled."

"Outside the Ark. But who can it be?"

"We must try to find out. It is an awesome thought that somewhere out there trained minds are trying to reach us."

"Beyond the eastern mountains. Oh, yes! That's what I feel all the time. The need to go out past those mountains. And I'm not going crazy. Someone really is trying to get in touch." She burst into thankful tears and felt a comforting arm around her shoulders.

"Now that's quite enough," the Initiator said firmly after a while. "Dry your eyes and listen to me. Obviously we can't keep you isolated from everyone in the Ark for ever, just so you can get a good night's sleep. But we do think it might be good for you to spend a couple of days and nights here, just to give you a rest. Then we've got work to do, my dear. And the first thing is for me to help train that undisciplined psyche of yours."

"You, Ma'am. Oh, my goodness!"

The Initiator laughed. "Being one of the Four doesn't exempt me from Ark work. For now, that work is going to be *you*. An Initiator is someone who starts a new idea, or a new way of looking at or doing things. We have never had a long-range receiver before, so the old rules and ways of learning simply don't apply. We will damp down that unruly PK of yours and concentrate on the long-range receiving. How does that sound?"

"Wonderful. Only, Ma'am . . ."

"What's the trouble?"

"If I'm to stay in the Black Hole, could I please be let out to go to the bathroom?"

The Initiator laughed. "There's a lavatory and a shower to your left directly outside the door. It was never locked, you know. You had only to turn the handle." She flicked Ruth under the chin. "You were so sure it was a prison, you never tried the door."

Ruth blushed. "But if it wasn't built as a prison . . . or a kind of punishment, what is it actually *for*?"

"When the Ark was designed it was realised that there

46

might be times when the leaders of the community might need to get together and discuss policy in private. As you know, the aim of the Ark has been to encourage high psychic abilities. But until a certain level of skill and trust had been developed there was literally no way of keeping secrets. That is why the Black Hole was built – as a discussion room, nothing more. Nowadays it isn't used, as we have better control over our minds. And of course, it is a severe deprivation for us, since once the door is shut we are completely cut off from the loving and protective force of the Web."

"So it never was a prison?"

"Of course not. Only a threat for naughty children. That was all that was ever needed." She laughed. "I don't know what we'll use now."

"What do you mean?"

"Everyone in the City knows you've been 'imprisoned' here. When you return to Web life they're going to be surprised that you look so well, that you were so untouched by the experience."

"I could bleach my hair white," suggested Ruth, enjoying the idea of returning to Grade Eight a broken spirit, aged beyond her years.

"I don't think we need go *that* far. But it might help if you refrained from mentioning just how comfortable you are."

"Leave it to me, Initiator, Ma'am."

So WHEN Ruth returned to class three days later, it was with a solemn face. She could feel the girls' questions battering her mind, but there was a new-found stillness inside her and she found it easier to push them aside than before.

As soon as the bell rang for the end of morning class they clustered around. "What was it like, Ruth? Do tell."

She shook her head. "It's too awful. I couldn't possibly. Anyway it's time to tidy up or we'll be late for dinner."

"You're to sit next to me," said Angela firmly. "Come on."

"And me," chimed in Charity.

"What about the rest of us? We want to hear about it, too."

"Grab that big circular table in the corner. Grace, you always look tidy. Run ahead and get it for us."

It was very sweet being swept along in the centre of the crowd, sitting between the two most popular girls in the school, having one's meal brought on a tray instead of having to line up for it and look for a vacant place in which to sit and eat in silence. It wasn't surprising that it went to Ruth's head.

"Well, go on," said Patience. "Tell us."

Ruth took a mouthful of soup, broke off a piece of soybread, popped it into her mouth and chewed it thoughtfully. "It really *is* black," she said at last.

"Go on."

"The floors, the walls, the ceiling. Even the couch. As black as night." She let her voice fall in a dramatic whisper and drank some more soup. The girls stared, their food untouched.

"Weren't you scared to death?"

"Terrified. I lay there, surrounded by this awful blackness, and after a while it seemed to me that a great knife was slowly descending from the ceiling, swinging to and fro like the pendulum of an olden days' clock. Closer and closer it seemed to come, until the knife was ready to slash me in two."

Charity screamed, then covered her mouth and giggled. People sitting close by turned round curiously and began to listen, edging their chairs closer.

"You're making it up," said Patience. "Aren't you?"

"I'm telling you what *seemed* to me to be happening. If you don't believe me you don't have to listen." I can't believe myself, thought Ruth. Talking back, to *them*.

"Shush, Patience. Go on, Ruth," Angela encouraged. "What happened next?"

Isn't that enough? thought Ruth. Then she remembered. "I felt as if this blackness, which in the beginning had seemed a very long way off, was coming closer and closer. As if the

48

walls were squashing me. And I just *knew*, without even having to look, that in the centre of the floor was a trap door, and that soon, very soon, it would suddenly open and drop me into the pit of fire far below."

There was silence. Even Angela had no words.

"And you were there for three whole days?" Someone asked at last.

"And nights," said Ruth cheerfully and went on with her dinner.

Teacher Jonson stopped at their table. "My goodness, girls. What slow eaters you are today. Hurry up now or you'll be late for Ark duty. Dishes today and there are all the tables to be scrubbed."

There was a groan. Dishes and scrubbing came low on the list of jobs that must be done to keep the city running.

"Oh, not you," Teacher Jonson added as Ruth jumped up and began to stack plates. "Leave that for the others. You're to report to the Initiator's office for special training."

Ruth tried to keep the smile from spreading across her face. "Sorry I can't stay to help. See you later." She ran out of the dining room feeling both triumphant and guilty at the awful stories she'd told. Though I *was* careful not to say that any of it actually happened, she told herself.

IT WAS her only moment of triumph. For the next four months she worked harder than she had done in her whole life before. She still had to attend regular classes and struggle with the daily practice making of the Web. Every other moment of her day was spent with the Initiator or her helpers.

It was lucky that the Initiator was a patient woman, because Ruth fought furiously at the bending of her psychic will to another's.

"Trust me," the Initiator would say, after the books had somehow been plucked off the shelves in her office and hurled across the room.

"I do. Honestly I do."

49

"Then *relax*. Remember the game you used to play in Grade One, where one of you was blindfolded and had to learn to fall backwards into the arms of another person? You didn't know that the other person would be there, but you trusted."

"Y . . . yes."

"Then trust me *now*. Let go, Ruth and let me in, or we can't even begin."

Ruth would try, but the second she felt the Initiator's psyche touch hers she would bristle up again.

"Just like a porcupine!" exclaimed the Initiator in disgust. Ruth went to the library to find out what a porcupine looked like. Prickly and difficult to love, she thought, as she looked at the pictures. That figures!

Slowly she learned that her mind wasn't terrible to look at. Little by little she let down her defences, though she never learned to like this mind mingling.

Other lessons were more fun. The one she liked the best consisted in doing what she had always loved, being alone in the Dome, in her favourite niche from which she could look straight across to the eastern mountains. She watched the green turn slowly to red and gold, and the colours vanish as the snow fell and the world Outside turned to black and white and grey.

Some days she was sent up to the Dome with a sketch pad and told to draw whatever came into her mind. At times she could only sketch exactly what she saw from her perch. But at times it was almost as if another hand took hold of the pencil and scribbled quick sketches. A girl and boy bent over a fish trap. An open meadow planted with neat rows of vegetables. A great fire with people singing and dancing around it. A face, brown skinned, with a dimple at a corner of the mouth and long red hair.

Sometimes one of the Custodian's blue uniformed Communicators would sit beside her, training her in the techniques of concentration, so that she might send her thought waves far over the snowy mountains, towards that great question mark that lay beyond. It was infuriating work, and she dreaded it, because there was no way of knowing if, *out there*, someone was receiving the messages she sent. Certainly she never got a reply.

Occasionally now, not only in her dreams, she had the strange feeling that, for just an instant, she was in someone else's mind. There was the image of a man dressed in red with a small camera strapped to the middle of his forehead. An older man, bowed down and hunch backed, but with keen eyes. A woman dressed in finely woven robes but with a head as bald and shiny as a peeled egg.

There were feelings, too, that suddenly swept over Ruth, and yet which she knew were not hers. Feelings of being trapped. Fear of loneliness. Of the future, which seemed, in this other person's eyes, to stretch into the distance like a grey fog. Above all there was a hunger for beauty.

After a time Ruth began to associate this feeling with the red-haired girl, the girl with the dimple. The girl with the hoe.

51

4
The New Year

JANUARY THE FIRST, 2147 AD. Ruth woke long before the official rising time and lay excitedly longing for the lights to come on. One by one the others awoke, until they were all alert and the room hummed busily with their psychic activity.

"Oh, this is ridiculous!" Angela's bed creaked and Ruth heard her feet pad across the floor. With a decisive snap the light went on.

The others sat up in bed, hugging their knees, their eyes sparkling with anticipation. This was *their* day, far more important than a birthday. Each of them had been born in 2132 and each had reached the magic age of fifteen – adulthood – during the last year. Today, in the presence of the whole Web, they would cease to be neophytes and be welcomed as members of the adult community of Ark Three. And, as if that in itself were not sufficient excitement, there was to be a banquet and, after the banquet, a dance. With *boys*.

"But if Fidelius doesn't ask me I shall just die . . ." said Charity suddenly, and even Ruth knew exactly what she'd been thinking.

She sighed. "I'm scared to dance. Suppose I fall over my feet? Worse, suppose I fall over *his*?"

"Whose, Ruth? Who do *you* fancy?" There was no mistaking the mocking tone in Angela's voice.

Ruth flushed. "Nobody."

"Oh, come on." There was a laughing chorus of protests.

"No, honestly." But am I weird about that too? she

wondered. Because she just wasn't interested in boys like Justin or Michael or even the black-browed Fidelius. Somewhere in her heart was an image, as foggy as an out-of-focus microreader, and the image was nothing like any of the Grade Eight boys.

"Anyway, I expect no one'll ask me to dance. But if they do – oh, dear, whatever shall I do?"

"You'll dance, Ruth. It's easy." Apparently regretting her scornful remark, Angela jumped off her bed and grabbed Ruth's hand. "Come on. Let's practise."

"Dum-de-dum, dum-de-dum." Between the rows of beds they danced. "No, relax. You're like a board. Pretend you're dancing by yourself."

Ruth closed her eyes. As Angela hummed, into her mind flashed a picture of a dark night and a fire. Of a song and people dancing.

"That's it. Not bad at all. Now just remember that *he*'s supposed to lead, except in the country dances."

"I like them. I don't feel so stupid."

"You shouldn't worry so much about what other people are thinking of you." Angela gave the self-confident smile of the beautiful and clever, who have never been put down by anyone. "Then you'll get on better. There, I hear the others getting up. Time for showers, girls."

THE MORNING crawled by in endless insignificant duties, but at last Ruth found herself sitting with all the Grade Eight classes in the front rows of the Assembly Hall. It was a beautiful room, painted in shades of gold that reminded her of the sunlit glade of her dreams. At the centre was a low platform with four seats on it, each facing outwards to a different quadrant of the room. Around the platform were circles of chairs, sufficient for the whole population of Ark Three. The circles were broken by four main aisles that divided the seating into four quadrants.

It looks rather like a Web already, thought Ruth, shivering

in anticipation, with the spokes reaching out to the edges of the room and the four seats at the centre that would become the nexus of power when the Great Pattern was made.

Ruth's class filled the first three rows of one section, with the girls placed in order of age, so that Constance, Faith, Honesty and Angela, whose birthdays fell in January and February, occupied the front row. She was in the middle of the third row, with Grace and Charity on either side of her. The girls of Grade Eight A were in the opposite quadrant, flanked on either side by the boys of B and D.

How nice we look, she thought, in our clean uniforms. This will be the very last day we wear pale green. From now on what will it be? Behind her were scattered all the colours of the community. It was like a meadow full of flowers, the blue, yellow and mauve dotted among the dark green of Communicators. There was a low buzz of conversation, but running through it was the tingling heady excitement of Togethering. It was already beginning.

Ruth shivered and her hands went up to run through her hair. Supposed she failed to mesh, to become part of the Web, now, at this crucial moment?

"Don't you dare!" hissed Charity. Ruth looked at her angrily, but Charity hadn't been intruding on her thoughts. She grabbed Ruth's hands and put them firmly back in her lap. "After all the trouble Angela and I went to, to get your hair to lie down neatly, you're not to lay one finger on it!"

"Sorry. I forgot. Oh, Charity, do I look all right?"

"Fine." Charity was trying to catch the attention of Fidelius, the dark-haired boy from the library. "I just can't wait till the dance. Five hours to go. I'll die!"

Dance? thought Ruth. If I can just get through the next two hours!

A stir went through the Assembly as the four elected leaders walked down the aisle towards the centre. The Protector was in gold to depict the concentration of healing power, the Custodian was tiny in her dark green, the colour of Esper

54

power, the Warden short, stocky, matter-of-fact in dark blue, to signify the passing on of knowledge and wisdom. Then there was the Initiator, strikingly tall and blonde, with a strong bony face, her purple a rich contrast to the others.

For the eighty-one neophytes this Assembly was their first. Even the bouncy Charity and the self-assured Angela stood in awe as the Four bowed to the community and took their places, each on one of the four seats that faced outward towards the people.

After a moment's vibrant silence the Protector stood, his arms outstretched. "People of the Web, greetings! We come together on the first day of the new year, 2147, to welcome a new class into the fullness of our community. Today these eighty-one youngsters will leave the world of childhood behind to become fully responsible members of the Ark, with all the headaches *that* entails!"

Everyone, except the neophytes, laughed at his little joke. He went on seriously. "We meet also to strengthen the Great Pattern which we have striven to perfect for the last one hundred and forty-one years, and also to retell our history and renew our mandate for a better world. This year something else will be added ... "

A shiver of interest ran through the room. What is going to be different? Ruth wondered.

" ... But more of that later," the Protector went on. "First, we must put our young neophytes out of their misery and begin the inauguration."

He sat down amid applause and the Warden rose and faced the Grade Eight A class. Their teacher came down the aisle and stood beside him, the colourful sashes over her arm.

Charity groaned and whispered. "Why did we have to be in C? It'll be hours before he gets to us. I know I'll die."

Me, too, thought Ruth. Her heart was pounding and she dug her nails into the palms of her hands. The sashes hanging loosely over the teacher's arm suddenly fluttered upwards, as if caught in an unexpected breeze. The Protector turned in his

55

seat and shot a warning look at Ruth. She unclenched her hands and took three deep breaths. The sashes hung still.

One by one the girls were called forward. As each stood before him the Warden placed across her shoulders a sash of the colour she would wear for the rest of her life: yellow for a Healer, blue for a Teacher, dark green for a Communicator.

When the twenty girls of Eight A had filed back to their places the boys of Eight B were called forward and in turn were accepted into the Community.

"Our turn next," whispered Charity. "Oh, I wonder what I'll be. It's so easy for Patience and Faith. They already know."

Ruth ran her tongue over her dry lips and tried to swallow. I'll never make it. I'm going to faint. She sat frozen in her seat until Grace poked her painfully in the ribs and she stumbled out into the aisle after Charity.

There were a few surprises. Everyone was sure Honesty would be made a Communicator, but she received the blue sash of Teacher. Charity herself was chosen as a Healer and her squeak of surprise sent a ripple of laughter around the Assembly.

Then it was Ruth's turn. As she stepped forward the Warden turned away. For one dreadful moment she thought this must be the sign of rejection, that she wasn't fit to take her place in the community. Her knees sagged and she felt Teacher Jonson's steady hand under her arm.

The Initiator stepped forward, her purple uniform shining splendidly under the lights. "It is not often that I have the pleasure of taking an active part in this ceremony," she said. "For mine is a silent work, the work of watching. I am here because every society, however great its intentions, needs checks and balances. Warden, Custodian, Protector. These are all words that speak of keeping safe, holding secure. But a society that does nothing more than hold onto what it believes is bound for self-destruction. To survive one must grow. To grow one must reach out. To reach out one must risk. My

56

position as the fourth is to remind you all of the necessity of risk taking. I am a goad."

Ruth felt the uneasy stir of the community around her. The Initiator went on. "Once in a while, perhaps no oftener than twice or thrice in a generation, a person is born into our community whose natural gifts seem out of tune with the rest. The obvious desire of the community is to get rid of the anomaly, to smooth it over, to make things comfortable once more. It is my job to see that this does not happen without due thought. To suggest to you all that these goads and prickles are necessary to our health as a community."

She's talking about *me*, Ruth realised in deepest shame. A goad. A prickle. Like the porcupine. She tried to stand tall and face the piercing eye of the woman who had been her teacher for the last four months.

"Such a case has arisen among this year's neophytes. There is a group so small that it is almost lost among the five thousand of us, a group of mavericks, with unusual and sometimes startling and uncomfortable gifts. Gifts, nevertheless, which are vital to the health of the Ark. We call these special people Innovators, and it is to this group that we warmly welcome our newest member – Ruth!"

The Initiator placed a mauve sash around Ruth's shoulders. She muttered thanks and stumbled back to her place next to Charity. She didn't see the expression of envy on Angela's face, nor the stunned looks of the others. The rest of the ceremony, as the twenty-one boys of Eight D were welcomed, passed in a blur. She sat, hands clasped, and the voice of the Warden faded away. The blue, green and gold danced in front of her eyes, blurring, changing . . .

She seemed to be sitting in a far larger room, with thousands and thousands of people. The colours around her were harsh, crimson, white and brown, and the feelings that washed over her were as inharmonious as the colours. In place of the central dais was a white cube of stone. Ruth saw, as if from a long way off, a brown-clad woman clutch the side

57

of the white stone and then sink slowly to the floor, leaving on the stone a stain of crimson blood . . .

"Ouch!" Ruth jumped. Charity was pinching her arm.

"Good grief! What a moment to go to sleep!"

"I wasn't . . . I don't think I was . . ." Ruth looked around in a daze, at the soft colours and happy faces. "Oh, I'm so glad I live here, Charity. Aren't you?"

"Where else could one live? You *are* strange."

As the youngest boy in Eight D returned to his place the Protector once more stood. "Let us now link hands with our neighbours and concentrate on completing the Web and strengthening the Great Pattern that is our reason for being."

Charity's hand was warm and moist in Ruth's icy one. She felt Grace clutch her other hand and realised that *they* were just as afraid of spoiling the pattern as she was. Out of her own unsureness she let comfort flow into them. The comfort flowed back. She began to feel warm. Her muscles relaxed. Her busy brain slowed. She no longer felt the weight of her body against the seat.

There was a sense of timelessness, and in this No-Time Ruth felt herself leave her body and hover beneath the ceiling of the great room. Below her she could see a gold light grow and strengthen. It flowed from the centre where the four sat, hands linked, in four great rays out to the corners of the room. Connecting these powerful lines were circles of bright gold that flowed around each circle of seats.

Ruth watched this energy shimmer and strengthen until a sudden anxious thought flashed into her mind. What am I doing up here? I'm supposed to be down there, concentrating with the others. At once she fell rapidly towards the ground. She had an instant's impression of a row of quiet blind faces. With a sudden shock she saw her own face. Then she was back inside her body.

"Welcome," a voice spoke in her head. "I am Luke, the last of the Innovators before you. I welcome you to the Web."

Then other voices followed Luke's, until Ruth had received

58

the greetings of every member of the community. She knew them and loved them and in turn reached out shyly to greet the members of her own class.

After a long time – or had any time passed at all? – the pattern slowly dissolved. The Web was broken, the closeness lost. Ruth sighed. I wish it could have lasted for ever. But I know it will return. I am a part of it. I *do* belong. Wonderingly she fingered her Innovator's sash.

The Custodian stood and began to read from a white and gold book. "Here is the history of Ark Three, to be read on the first day of each year," she began, and they settled back to listen.

"In the beginning of the Age of Confusion that followed the End of Oil, the Arks were built by different faculties of the University in an attempt to protect the knowledge and wisdom of humankind, which was in danger, as in times before, of being totally lost.

"We in the Humanities were charged with guarding and developing our skills in communication and understanding, so that once the Age of Confusion was past there might be once more an Age of Peace, with no more wars and no more destruction of either people or natural resources through personal greed.

"One hundred and forty-one years have passed since the Arks were built. During this time we have concentrated all our energies on developing our skills in telepathy, healing and empathic communication. We have developed a society in which everyone has an equal opportunity, and in which the dull, the rough, the unpleasant work is shared by all, including the leaders. In the same way each of us bears an equal responsibility in the growth and development of the Web and the Great Pattern."

The Custodian closed the book and spoke clearly to the hushed assembly. "The Protectors, the Custodians, the Wardens who came before your present leaders had a clear mandate, when the Age of Confusion threatened the existence

59

of civilization. That mandate has been observed. We have protected the best in humanity. But, as the Initiator has told you, a society fully occupied with holding on to what it has can never survive. For a hundred and forty-one years we have consolidated, we have strengthened our powers. You have all felt the power of the Web, and strength of the Great Pattern. Well, then, be ready. The time has come to risk!"

She sat down amid a buzz of excited conversation. "Risk?" "What kind of risk?" "What can she mean?"

The Initiator rose again. "Friends, I share your concern. There have been fourteen Initiators since the founding of the Ark. I am the fifteenth to wear the purple. I am also the first to stand before you and say that I truly believe that the time has come for us to move."

"To move where?"

"What's wrong with the Ark the way it is?"

"Newness for the sake of newness?" One voice spoke louder than the rest and the babble died down. "You are young, Initiator. Respectfully, perhaps . . . "

The Initiator smiled. "It is a fair comment, my friends. I *am* young. I have held this office for just six years. If the suggestion for change had come from me you would be justified in challenging me personally. But it does not. It comes from Outside. During the last six months we have received messages – garbled and indistinct as yet – but clear enough to lead us to believe that, not far away, there is another Ark whose people have also developed telepathic skills. Imagine: a whole other community with whom we can communicate, whom we can trust. Who can trust us. With whom we can work."

There was a buzz of excited chatter. *Outside*, thought Ruth. Her heart leapt. Maybe at last they'll let me go Outside.

The Initiator's quiet voice, through its very quietness, overcame the excitement. The Assembly silenced and she went on. "As you know the University made five separate attempts, working in entirely different directions, to save the knowledge of humankind. It was decided that each Ark should be entirely independent, with no communication between them. So, if one failed or was overcome by the forces of the rabble, the others might still survive intact. Remember, too, that the attempt by *our* University was only one of many different plans developed by people scattered across the country. But in all these years, nearly a century and a half, we have not heard a word from any of these groups, either from our own University or from beyond. Not until recently. Last August."

Last August. But that was when ... a terrifying thought crept into Ruth's mind. She pushed it away and forced herself to go on listening.

"The communications all seem to be coming from beyond the eastern mountains. We believe that there *are* foundations in that direction. We are searching the archives at this time to find what information we can. But the evidence is there. We are not alone."

The audience roared and clapped. In the midst of the excited tumult, in spite of the fact that she was clapping her own hands until the palms stung, Ruth found her mind standing back critically and asking: Will we be able to start learning all over again? If a Web of five thousand was difficult to achieve, how about one twice as big, or even bigger? Suddenly, into her mind flashed the terrifying picture of a woman in brown crumpled at the foot of the white stone. And blood everywhere.

The Initiator had begun to talk again and Ruth pushed the horrible picture to one side of her mind and made herself concentrate.

"Today is New Year's Day. A new year indeed! A very different year it may turn out to be. But you've all sat still for long enough. Today is a time for rejoicing. Starting to-morrow there will be special study sessions. You will all have the opportunity of studying the evidence and discussing it among yourselves and with us. We will, of course, make no important decisions without a consensus."

The Warden then stood. "In half an hour we will meet for the celebration banquet, after which there will be the dance that all you young people have been waiting for."

"I wonder what evidence they have of someone out there," Charity said as they walked towards the dormitory.

Ruth bit her lip. What would the girls think when they found that it had begun with *her*? She forced herself to smile. "Well, now we're full members of the community we'll have a chance to find out. It's very exciting, isn't it?"

But Charity didn't answer. They had just reached the door of the dormitory. "Oh, look."

There on each bed lay their new uniforms, each in the appropriate new colour.

"And I must say," said Angela generously. "That you look quite nice in that shade of mauve, Ruth. It makes your eyes look green instead of that funny muddy shade."

Then Charity said, "Don't forget, Angela, that we've decided to ask Ruth to share the room with Faith and us."

It really is the best day of my whole life, thought Ruth, as she smoothed down her unruly hair.

5
Outside?

IN KINDERGARTEN and Grade One jigsaw puzzles were used as part of Esper training, five children working together to complete a puzzle by pooling their mental resources. The next six months' work was like the putting together of such a giant jigsaw. The pieces came to Ruth randomly, many making no sense at all; yet, at the end of six months a picture of Outside must emerge.

A paper from Archives. Yellowed, worn at the folds, it was a picture of folded mountain ranges washed in with a grey-brown colour, the whole criss-crossed with wriggling red lines and networked with fine black ones. Like a random kind of Web, Ruth thought.

"What exactly is it?"

"A road map of this region, from the Days of Oil. Ruth, I want you to look at this map and think about it. Tell us, if you can, where your dreams come from."

"I can't. Not possibly. How should I know? It's only a piece of paper. From behind the eastern mountains. That's all I can tell you." Ruth's voice went up and she could feel her muscles tighten nervously. She could tell from the Initiator's face just how much she wanted an answer.

"Hey now, don't stiffen up like that." The Initiator's voice was gentle. "Just relax. Breathe slowly." Skilful fingers kneaded her shoulder muscles. She felt her stomach muscles unknot and her eyelids droop.

Her right hand stretched out. Like a magnet the map

63

drew her hand. Her finger pointed. "There. Right there."

SHE MET LUKE, the youngest Innovator next to her, twenty years old, with smooth brown hair and twinkling dark eyes. He showed her a sketch map. It had been hastily drawn, the names scribbled in, and it had no title.

"This was in the Archives, too. Look, Ruth. Exactly the place you marked on the other map."

She looked past his pointed finger at a mountainous area, a river, a small circle. Printed beside the circle were the words 'Ark One'.

ARK ONE. Now the dream had a name and a direction. The Expedition to Ark One. Plans became more concrete. Ruth's notebook of sketches became public property among the planners. They riffled through her pages, arguing with each other, turning to her for clarification. "Exactly what clothes do they wear Outside?"

Ruth remembered the red-haired girl. "A fur tunic and trousers. Fur slippers indoors and for outdoors, fur boots tied around the leg with string – or something like string."

"Fur? We cannot be expected to slaughter fur-bearing animals!"

"I am sure that the chemists can come up with some other insulating material."

"But will we need that much? We don't plan to leave until June."

"In summertime they wear short tunics and have bare legs and feet," Ruth put in helpfully.

"Bare feet? We wouldn't last a day like that."

"In fact boots may be the most crucial item of clothing."

"Made to fit each person precisely . . ."

". . . out of synthetic strong enough for rock climbing."

"And we should probably have rainproof coats."

"But the rain . . ." Ruth remembered a dream of standing in a forest glade with the rain coming softly through the trees.

She could still feel the sweetness of it on her cheeks, her eyelids, her open mouth. "Rain is lovely," she said. "Why do we need raincoats?"

"Perhaps the people of Ark One are accustomed to Outside and move freely to and fro. But we – we are disgustingly weak. We'd probably catch pneumonia."

The people of Ark One! What were they really like? How did they live? As the weeks passed they began to assume the stature of the heroes and heroines of the old myths and sagas.

FOR FIVE months Ruth had been free of the nightmare. At the full moon of the vernal equinox it began again. She felt that she was struggling through the dark with some incredibly heavy load on her shoulder. She could feel it cut her muscles as she climbed up a steep place – was it a staircase? Then the real horror began. She was crawling across a narrow bridge, dragging the heavy object after her. It was night and there were no lights anywhere. There was a continuous roaring sound, like peal after peal of thunder, but no rain. She was swallowed up in fear. Fear of falling, fear of heights, fear of being found out. But by whom, or for doing what she did not know.

She awoke, screaming, to find Faith holding her and shaking her. Doors slammed. Glass broke.

"I'm sorry." Ruth shivered at the memory. "I didn't mean to . . ."

Angela groaned and put her pillow over her head, but Faith whispered, "It's all right. Don't worry," and held her hand until she fell asleep again.

Next day the dream was taken apart. After a morning of answering questions and drawing pictures Ruth was exhausted and discouraged. The only thing they had found out for certain was that the object she had dreamed of carrying was an agricultural instrument known as a hand plough, probably used for the cultivation of grain.

"Grain? I don't remember that. I've dreamed of them

growing vegetables Outside, but for the most part they seem to rely on berries and nuts and roots and . . . and meat."

"Meat? Are you sure?"

Ruth remembered the hunting dream. It must have occurred in early winter, because there was a scatter of snow on the leaves that lay brown and gold on the ground. Among the shadows of the trees she had seen the shadow of hunters, silent, waiting. Then, among the branches a movement of great beasts, three of them, looking as if *they* had branches on their heads.

"But perhaps that was just the dream."

"No, they would be elk," a teacher biologist had said, when she had drawn them.

In the quietness of her dream had suddenly come a sound barely louder than the silence, a high faint singing that pierced the ear. Two of the three animals fell with a great crash into the underbrush. The third bounded into the shadows and was gone.

The next part of the dream wasn't nice, and Ruth hated having to remember it. There were people with knives, slicing and tearing at the brown hairy skin; blood spurting, oozing, dark and sticky against the snow and the leaves. Grey guts spilling steaming onto the cold ground. And laughter. Song and laughter.

WHAT WERE the people of Ark One really like? They seemed to be a mass of contradictions, living in a domed city, and yet in wooden houses in the forest, culturing yeast proteins and yet killing for food.

"We shouldn't be disgusted," Karol, one of the historian Teachers, argued. "Meat has been part of human diet since the Ice Age. It was a necessary part of our development. The concentrated protein gave human beings time to think, to create, to become more than grazers whose whole life was filled with the process of finding enough food to survive."

"But nowadays, when it is no longer necessary – why

would they? Do you suppose they will expect us to . . .? It is unthinkable. It would be a denial of our philosophy to take life."

"We *must* accept the people of Ark One as we find them," Luke argued. "After all, the original idea of separate Arks was that each should develop independently, so that each group should bring its own particular strength to the making of a new world."

"By killing defenceless animals?"

"We don't have to hunt, ourselves. We will take a supply of soy cakes and dried yeast and vegetable soups and stews."

"Some of the currants and grapes from the Dome garden should be ripe by then. We can have dried fruit, too."

"Food for fourteen days! That will be quite a load."

"We can fish," Ruth suggested, remembering dreams of lines and hooks, of traps built of willow branches. She remembered savouring the smell as she woke. "It's not really like meat."

Everyone else agreed and a team went down to the stores to investigate. They came back triumphantly with fishing rods and line, and tiny bundles of feather and silk concealing wicked-looking hooks.

The historians were fascinated and wasted so much line, with such danger to each other's eyes, that the Warden decreed that casting must only be practised by one person at a time in a vacant room. "Or we'll be blinded before we even set out."

BY APRIL plans were going well and the time had come to choose the twenty who would go. This was a number thought to be sufficiently large to mesh with each other and so maintain their Esper strength, but not so large as to seem threatening to the people of Ark One.

The very notion of making contact with another telepathic group was a challenge even to the most retiring, and there were hundreds of volunteers.

Ruth must go, of course, it was decided, and the Initiator and at least one other Innovator, since they alone had the natural skill to react quickly to the unexpected. There must be a team of Healers in case of accident or illness, and an expert in geology and natural history. Above all, the twenty must contain the strongest Communicators in Ark Three.

"We must be able to reach out to them as soon as possible, to let them know that we are on the way. And, of course, it is essential that we keep our contact with the Web."

Contact with the Web. Slowly people began to understand that keeping in contact was not going to be the same thing as being a *part* of the Web. To leave the Ark and the protection of the psychic force that had bound them together since childhood was terrifying.

"Not everyone can cope with that loneliness." The Initiator shook her head. "But how can we find out before it's too late? We can't afford to carry even one psychic wreck on such a rough journey."

"Why don't you put them in the Black Hole?" asked Ruth, half joking.

The Initiator stared and laughed. "What an excellent idea! We will start immediately screening all the volunteers, beginning with Luke and myself. For if we should fail, I don't have much hope for the rest."

As a means of eliminating volunteers the Black Hole was a great success. It was a shock to see a senior member of the community run for the door, pull it open and stagger into the corridor outside, sweating and shivering with fear at the momentary loss of contact with the Web. Even the company of two or three others was often not enough to make up for the absence of its psychic force – the terrible loneliness.

After the testing the team was chosen. Paola, the chief Healer, was forty-five. Under her guidance were Healers Miriam, Raef and Grayle. The chief Communicator was Thomas, with a team of Crystal, Helen, Olga, Gil, Basil and Valentine. Three Teachers were picked, Athena, a biologist,

Bryan, a geologist and Karol, the historian who had been the most help in the early stages of planning.

Among all these experts Ruth began to feel lonely. The nearest in age to her was Luke, the other Innovator, but he was a fully-fledged member of the community, the only psychokinetist and the map-maker of the expedition, too.

"But without you there wouldn't *be* an expedition," Luke consoled her.

"So if things go wrong you'll know who to blame, huh?"

He laughed. "But if you feel that you're useless, let's do something about it. There's plenty of time before June to develop your kinetic powers. We'd make a good team."

"Do you think I really could?" Ruth looked doubtful.

"Don't be so negative. For a girl who slammed doors and broke dishes all over the Ark . . . ."

"But that wasn't really kinetic power."

"Of course it was. But misdirected, like a baby's muscles, all over the place."

"Thanks a lot!"

"Come on. Let's make a start."

He laid a pencil on its side on the table. "Now roll it off."

Ruth concentrated. "I can't!"

"Relax. Don't breathe so hard."

"I am relaxed," she said between her teeth. She felt a sudden flare of anger at her own stupidity and the pencil rolled from the table to the floor.

"I did it!"

"So you did. Now pick it up."

She leaned forward.

"No, not with your hand. With your *mind*."

Ruth concentrated on the stupid pencil for what seemed like hours. It lay on the floor like a – like a pencil. "Oh, this is hopeless!"

"Will you allow me to enter your mind?" Luke asked formally.

69

"Yes, if you can get through."

He laughed. "I've heard of your reputation for stubbornness."

She tensed and then tried to relax. After all, I was able to let the Initiator in, she told herself.

She felt a mind guide her mind, as a teacher helps a child form its first letters. Gently he showed her how to direct the molecules that made up the pencil, so that they moved together in one direction. The pencil trembled, stood on end, lifted back to the table top.

"I did it. I actually did it!"

"Do it again, then." Luke knocked the pencil to the floor. And, after a struggle, she succeeded.

"Lesson number one," Luke said quietly as she sat back in her chair, beaming. "To knock down is easy. All it takes is a flash of anger. But to build and lift requires concentration and energy. And skill. Do you want to learn it?"

"Oh, yes please."

They practised daily, after all the other work was done, when Ruth was sometimes so tired that she did not know where, inside herself, she would find one single gram of energy. But Luke kept her at it and her skill improved. He seemed to understand her fear of failure, and their lessons were kept a secret.

PERHAPS HE *did* talk to the Initiator about her feelings, for one day she called Ruth into her office.

"There are still three places to fill on the team. Would you like to have friends from your own class?"

"Oh, yes, thank you. That would make all the difference. But maybe they won't want to go."

"You can but ask."

Ruth needn't have worried. Charity and Faith jumped at the idea. Even Angela. As for the others, they pestered her constantly.

"I'd be much better than Charity. After the first two

kilometres you'll have to carry her."

"No, Ruth. Take me."

"Me, please. I want to go."

"You'll have to do your stint in the Black Hole, like the others. Two days and nights away from the Web. Let's see if Angela and Faith and Charity make it."

Ruth blushed with pleasure. They *wanted* to go with *her*.

The next day the girls were put to the test. "I don't know if I can." Faith hesitated outside the door.

"There's nothing to it," Ruth pleaded. "And I'll stay with you all the time, honest."

"Come on you two." Angela stuck her chin up and pulled open the heavy door. "The other girls will never let us forget it if we don't at least try."

Faith looked as if she didn't care what the others thought. Angela pushed them into the room ahead of her. Ruth followed and shut the door.

Faith put her hands to her ears. "It's so silent. I feel as if I've gone deaf."

"And it's cold." Charity shivered.

Ruth laughed. "It's the same temperature as the rest of the Ark, honestly it is."

"Well, I'm freezing."

Angela ignored their complaints and walked boldly round the room, touching the black walls. She stared up at the black ceiling and down at the black floor. "You lied to us, Ruth!"

"What are you talking about?"

"All that stuff about knives and the fiery pit in the floor. I just knew it was a story."

Ruth blushed and then laughed. "I'd forgotten about that. Actually it *was* a story. A story I'd read, and I kept thinking, what if this were to happen? Well, it was very brave of you to come in here, remembering that. So now you know there's nothing to worry about. All the other members of the team went through it and came out healthy and sane, didn't they?"

"Ye . . s. But an awful lot of people didn't make it."

"You just have to open the door if you can't bear it," Ruth said gently. "But I hope you don't have to. You'll be such good company on the trip."

She saw a peculiar expression flash across Angela's face. What was it? She was still no good at empathising with other people's feelings, though her kinetic powers were growing stronger every day. Faith and Charity were looking embarrassed, as if they *had* caught Angela's unspoken message. There was a silence.

"Well, shall we play cards or do a puzzle? Something to pass the time and take your mind off the room," she suggested; and the rest of the day passed amicably enough. But Ruth woke in the middle of the night to hear someone crying softly.

She sat up in the darkness. "Who is it? Can I help?"

The crying stopped and there was silence. Was it Faith? Or Charity? Next morning they looked quite cheerful. Surely it couldn't have been Angela? Angela, the strong one, the leader.

She had woken feeling that something was missing. She was certainly not missing the Web. She puzzled over it through the day and realised at last that she was actually missing her dreams. The sense of that other person far away, joined to her by a gossamer thread. For the first time she put a name to the unknown fellow dreamer: Tomi. And then she thought, I wonder how I know?

I miss you, Tomi, she said to herself. But it won't be long before we meet. I wonder what you're like? As handsome as Luke? A telepath or a healer?

Two months to wait. Two months for the snow to melt and the land to dry up. And then . . .

ONCE THE TWENTY had been chosen there was little more time to count the days. They rushed by, packed with new experiences. At first, dressed in their everyday uniforms, they walked the long circular passages of the Ark. The outermost passage was just over three kilometres in length. Four times around, it had been suggested, might be equivalent to a day's march. It took them a week just to be able to walk the distance.

Then they began to climb the never-used emergency stairs that ran between each floor at the extremity of each of the four quadrants. They learned to walk up the sixteen metres from the generator and water treatment plant past the storage bays, the living quarters, and the manufacturing and food processing floors to the level of the Dome, ground level, and then jog the seven hundred and eighty-five metres to the next stairway and go down again.

They did it, gasping and stopping after every ten stairs. They did it, resting at the end of each flight. Over and over, up the stairs, along the passages and down again, until they could climb up and down all four staircases without losing breath. Their muscles became firm and hard. They felt confident.

Then they were fitted out with boots and rainproof jackets and a fifteen kilo pack and it all began again. Panting up the stairs, resting on the landings, stumbling along the perimeter corridor to the next flight down.

They groaned at the aches and the stiffness. They lay in hot tubs and had the knots massaged out of their painful legs by teams of Healers. They lay under sun lamps slowly accustoming their skins to the sun that, for the last six generations, had reached them only through the plastic of the Dome.

By June even a stranger could have picked out the twenty from the other five thousand inhabitants of Ark Three. They stood taller. Their bodies were muscled and alert and their eyes had a snap to them. Their skins had changed too, to a deep tan on dark haired people like Luke, to a golden hue on the Initiator and many of the others, all the way down to Charity's freckles.

"I look crazy," wailed Charity, counting the dots across the

73

bridge of her nose in a mirror. "He'll hate me. Do you suppose they'll fade when this is all over and we're safely home?"

But she felt better when a new fashion sprang up among the neophytes and younger adults, of pencilling dots on their cheek bones with brown crayons.

"HOW MANY PEOPLE live in Ark One?"

"Who are their leaders?"

"Can't you give us any more details?"

For the hundredth time Ruth was in conference with the Four. She shook her head. "I'm sorry. I just don't have those kind of answers. I know you gave me a list of things to think about before I went to sleep and I have tried. Yes, my dreams are still going on. But it's as if no one was listening. I dream, but I'm getting no useful information. I don't even know if Ark One looks like this . . . except for that one room." She fell silent, remembering the huge Assembly, the white stone and the blood. No one had understood the meaning of that dark dream. The stone like an altar. And blood. Human sacrifice? The idea was unthinkable . . .

"But you *are* still dreaming?"

"Oh, yes. Just as I did before. Two kinds of dreams. One is more like a message than the other. It's as clear as if I were watching a video, clearer, because I'm inside it, part of it. Most of the dreams are about outdoors. They are all beautiful, with meadows and forests and a wide river, much bigger than our little one. I feel happy and free in those dreams and I wake up feeling good inside myself."

"Do you see the same people? Do you recognise them?"

"Oh, yes." Ruth grabbed a piece of paper and began to draw. "This man is older than the others and I sense that he's recently suffered a great deal, but that he too is now free and happy. Then there's this couple. I guess they must be about forty years old. And this girl is their daughter, I think."

"I recognise her." The Warden stabbed his finger on the paper. "I've seen her before."

74

"She's the girl with the hoe, the red-haired girl. She seems to be very important in the dreams, as if she were the leader . . ."

"Go on."

"When she appears in the dreams I feel that she's someone I once knew and loved very much. And that she's gone. Perhaps she's dead. Yet I keep feeling that I must go and look for her. I'm sorry. It's awfully muddled."

"I wish we knew what they were really like. For all we know they may have reverted to some savage state and that is why they wear furs instead of synthetic."

"What a macabre fancy, Initiator. Surely they must be at a high level of development, since they're able to communicate with us – better, I say, than we can communicate with them."

The Warden smiled drily. "That's the point, isn't it? *Are* they communicating with us? It seems sometimes that they are just broadcasting at large, since Ruth alone is able to pick up their messages, if messages they are."

"Is it really likely that they are savages?"

"No. But who could have forecast the horrors of the Age of Confusion? Who would have thought that human beings could so quickly lose their grip on the civilization of thousands of years?"

"True, Initiator. Go on, Ruth. I'm sorry I interrupted."

"I mentioned two dreams, Warden. In the second kind I get no clear pictures. They are distorted and scary, and I seem to be inside this person – Tomi."

"Is she a person of your own age, do you know?"

"She's not a woman at all. A man, a bit older than me, I think, but not as old as Luke."

"To be totally at one in the mind of a person of the other sex is difficult. That is, perhaps, why the dreams are muddled and nightmarish. What is this Tomi like?"

"I don't think he's very tall. He wears rather grand robes, all decorated along the hem, rather like the pictures of ancient

75

Romans, you know. But I've never seen him look in a mirror, so I don't know what he looks like, of course."

"And what actually happens, when you're in his body?"

"I dream of falling. Of drowning. Of crawling across a narrow bridge in a storm – I can hear the wind and the thunder. Sometimes I see other people, through his eyes, I suppose. There are men in red and things strapped to their foreheads. And there's one man who seems to be special. But ..."

"What is it?"

"Maybe I'm getting it wrong, but it seems that there's something wrong with all their backs."

"Something *wrong*?"

"As if they were hunchbacked."

"How very odd."

"Do you suppose ... some genetic weakness?"

"In only a hundred and forty years – it couldn't possibly become so widespread. I expect it's just a dream aberration. Nothing to worry about."

"I hope you're right, Warden." The Initiator frowned.

Ruth shivered.

"What is it, my dear?"

"Suppose we get there and find they are like that, savage and deformed. Or suppose we go east all that way across the mountains, and when we arrive, there's nothing there at all. You're building so much on my dreams. *Mine*. It'll be my fault."

"It most certainly won't be. The choice to go was the result of a free and open vote. And you're not alone this time. You're part of a team, with the Initiator in charge. The final decisions will be hers. You have a skilled map reader in Luke. There is a powerful team of Communicators along. And there is the Web, to support you all as long as we can reach you. I am confident that as you get closer to the Ark the signals will get clearer and the Communicators will be able to get in touch. Why, I shouldn't be surprised if, by the time you sight

Ark One, they are not all out there, ready to welcome you with open arms. After all, their signals wouldn't be so powerful if they didn't want to get in touch with someone."

To get in touch, thought Ruth. Tomi, are you really out there?

6

To the Mountains

THE SNOW melted and the river swelled with the run–off from the mountains. The grass greened and the trees unfurled their leaves. Colour once more dotted the meadowland that stretched westward and southward. The days lengthened and everyone was ready.

Then, on April the twenty-eighth, it began to rain. Not a thunder shower or a spring sprinkling, but a steady unrelenting downpour that persisted day after day. Water streamed from the curved plastic of the Dome. Ruth could hardly see the drowned world beyond. The river spilled over its ancient banks. Along the corridors and up and down the stairs the team of twenty walked, afraid of losing their new-found strength, in an agony of impatience to be off.

On June the second the rain stopped, as abruptly as if a tap had been turned. The clouds rolled eastward and the sun shone down brilliantly on the wet and steaming land.

"Tomorrow?" begged Ruth. The Four shook their heads. Bryan, the geologist, agreed with them.

"Look at those hills. See the white threads among the folds? Every one of those threads is a freshet scouring down the slope, swelling the streams, making the rivers impassable. There are other dangers after a rain like that: rockfalls, mud-slides. We would be crazy not to wait."

"I'm going crazy waiting! Suppose it starts raining again?" Ruth found it hard to cope with the prickliness that was growing inside her. She needed so badly to reach out to this unknown person – no, these two people – the one in whom she dreamed, Tomi, and the other, the girl with red hair. Her feelings were like a bitter hunger that with each day grew more intense. She could feel them drawing her towards them and she could feel her body respond to the pull. "What if it rains?" she wailed again.

"Then we must wait," answered Bryan, as stolid as the rocks he studied.

But it didn't rain. Each day dawned clear and then grew misty as the hot sun sucked the moisture out of the ground in smoky tendrils. By noon it was clear again and at night the stars shimmered from horizon to horizon.

Early on the morning of June the eighth, 2147, the community of Ark Three met for a final Togethering. Around the Assembly, down the aisles and into the centre the Web wove itself in a golden thread that became complete in the nexus of the Four.

The power of the Web poured love and strength into the twenty who were about to set out into the unknown. Even Ruth, isolated from its full power by her different psyche, felt her throat tighten at the kindness that wrapped itself around her like arms, that warmed her like the fires of her dreams . . .

And now, in response to her dreams, the twenty left the Assembly, though not yet the fulness of the Web, and walked silently to the elevator and up to the first floor beneath the Dome. Silently they shouldered their packs and trudged along the corridor to the tunnel entrance.

One by one they passed through the Door and climbed the ladders, to stand in knee-high grass under the wide clear sky. The last to climb out was Karol. He let the lid fall shut with a final thud.

They looked at each other uneasily. How huge the sky was. How vast the grassland. Charity bit her lip and looked as if she were about to cry. But the Web was still there to comfort them. The group was like a creature that had remained encysted underground for years and years. Now it had put forth a single tendril, a pseudopod, to explore the new environment. But it was still part of the main body. It was still safe.

"Come on," said Ruth. She shouldered her pack and began to walk.

The beginning of their march led south into the grassland, with the mountain range some three kilometres to the left. The sun was high, slightly to their left and in front of them, and it cast a golden dazzle across the high grass, so that it seemed that they were wading through a green gold sea.

The air was clean and heavy with the scent of clover. Bees blundered drunkenly from flower to flower and dragonflies stitched blue and bronze patterns through the air. Ruth felt the tension fall from her shoulders like a cast-off load. She walked with a spring, in spite of the pack she carried. She looked sideways at Luke and saw that he, too, was smiling.

After an hour they bore south-east. The long grass was replaced by a short wiry ground cover of creeping plants and low wiry shrubs. At first the walking was easier, since now they could see where they were putting their feet, but slowly the ground began to rise, more and more steeply, until they found that they were having to stop and catch their breath and rub cramped leg muscles.

At noon the Initiator called a halt for lunch. They all collapsed thankfully onto the short turf. The meal was a silent one. All of them were busy with their thoughts. Each of them looked back, from time to time, towards that curve of the Dome that shone silver under the noon sun. Six kilometres away it lay, like a silver lens in the grass. The Web was growing weaker now. It was hard to hold on to. Soon it would be gone. So they were silent.

Only Ruth was not concerned with the Web. She looked eagerly eastward towards the mountains. They seemed to roll on for ever, like a dark tree-covered ocean. Somewhere there . . . but how could Luke lead them to the exact spot?

"Where are you?" she said softly, so the others could

not hear. "Who are you, Tomi? And why do you call to me?"

The hills and mountains were silent. No psyche reached out to meet hers. Only a little breeze riffled the grassland that lay like a broad lake between the foothills and the mountains.

By midafternoon they had turned due east. Now the Ark was out of sight and ahead of them lay thirty kilometres of grassland. On its verge they made camp for the night.

The low brush provided plenty of dead wood for their fire. They scraped a place free of vegetation and surrounded it carefully with stones. At the touch of a match the fire crackled and sent sparks shooting up into the sky. The living flame was like a kind of magic to them. Its cheerful noise thrust back the silence of the empty world.

From a small stream they drew water for cooking. Then they washed their blistered feet. The Healers anointed and bandaged them and laid their hands on them. Soon the redness and the throbbing lessened.

"But we have to be more careful. If you feel a wrinkle in a sock stop at once and take your boot off and smooth it out," Paola warned. "We'll be useless lame."

"How far did we walk today?" Angela asked.

"About fourteen kilometres," said Luke.

"How far do we have to go?"

"Perhaps another hundred."

"A hundred!" Their heads all turned, as if pulled by an invisible thread, to look at the dark line to the east.

"We'll never make it," Charity said despairingly.

"Yes, we will. It's going to be all right," Ruth said. "We're not accustomed to it yet, that's all. Each day will be easier."

The Initiator jumped to her feet. "Ruth's right. And what we need now is a hot meal. Who's got today's dinner in their pack? All right, Helen, get it out. The water's almost boiling. It'll be ready in no time. And afterwards we'll make our own Web. That's all that's really wrong. We're missing the Web."

So, after a stew of dried vegetables and yeast cakes, they

rinsed the plates and tidied up the camp site. Then they made up the fire and sat around it, holding hands, concentrating their forces. Slowly, waveringly, the Web rebuilt itself, a poor weak thing compared with the wonder of the Web of the whole community, but nevertheless a Web.

"None of us is alone," said the Initiator softly, as they sat with the firelight dancing on their faces. "We have each other. Together we will be strong. Together we will succeed."

Sleep came slowly that first night in spite of their fatigue. In her tent with Angela, Faith, Charity and the Initiator, Ruth lay rigid, listening to the crackle of cooling embers and the whisper of wind across the grass. A stone at the edge of the fire suddenly exploded and they all sat up, stared wildly at each other, and sheepishly lay down again. An owl drifted by, its eerie hunting call scaring them all again. Ruth shivered. It had seemed such a great adventure, back under the Dome.

She fell asleep at last and dreamed that she was in Tomi's body, sleeping on the hard ground under the stars without even a blanket. Hungry and cold. Friendless and alone. She woke in cold despair and sat up, shivering. It was all right. There, around her, were the huddled shapes of her sleeping friends. She wasn't alone. The wind shook the synthetic cloth of the tent, but it could not penetrate it. She snuggled into her sleeping bag and slept without dreams until dawn.

For the whole of that day they trudged eastwards across the grassy plain. Slowly the mountains crept closer. By evening they were less than six kilometres away. During the morning they had stumbled across a strange line, running as straight as a ruler from north to south. When Bryan scraped away the meagre soil he found a black hard surface.

"It must be a road," he said. "See how straight it runs."

"From the olden days." Ruth touched it warily.

"Imagine the cars," said Karol, "travelling at a hundred kilometres an hour on roads like this, criss-crossing the country. People on the move. All the time moving."

"I wonder why?"

They stared at the green line that ran like a thread across the expanse of grassland.

"If only we could find a road going east we could make much better time. This moss and short grass is like a carpet to walk on."

But after Luke had consulted his maps he shook his head. "The roads seem to run mostly north and south, the way most of the valleys go. Nobody would build a road over the top unless they had to. And this is all wilderness park. I mean it was. Back then."

They crossed the road and ploughed on through the high grass. Later that afternoon they crossed another road. It was the last sign of the old civilization that they were to see for days.

As the sun set and the sky slowly darkened, the stars began to appear. "See over there in the east." Luke pointed. "Those three bright stars that form a triangle. So long as we see them ahead of us we'll be heading in the right direction. Below them there is a neck between two mountains. Do you see it? Tomorrow we'll be up there. Tomorrow we'll see the way ahead more clearly."

See our way more clearly. Ruth envied Luke's certainty. But then he had the maps. All she had was a shifting kaleidoscope of dreams. Turn them this way and a pattern emerged. Turn them again and the fragments would form a shape with a quite different meaning.

Suppose I'm wrong? Suppose the Four were wrong to believe in my dreams? Maybe it's all in my head and I'm leading them into the wilderness. To starvation and death.

That night she twisted and turned, slept and woke and slept again only fitfully. The next day, as they climbed slowly up towards the high pass between the even higher ranges, her thoughts pounded in her head. Suppose I'm wrong? Suppose...

As the way grew steeper the scatter of great beech and maple trees gave way to close-set hemlock and pine. Beneath their shade it was almost chilly. A sudden rattle directly overhead startled them all. They froze. A small rusty grey animal with a bushy tail scuttled down a tree trunk and leapt across to another.

"It's all right," Athena's voice quivered. "It's a squirrel, that's all. Just a squirrel."

"If that's the biggest creature we meet I guess we have nothing to worry about," Angela joked.

"I'm surprised we didn't meet elk and deer crossing the grassland. Up here I'd expect to find bear."

"Are they dangerous?"

"Who knows? Our information is a hundred and forty years out of date. Perhaps with fewer people, less pressure and no pollution, their habits may have changed."

"And if they haven't?"

"Short-sighted and bad tempered. If we see any signs of their presence we should make a lot of noise. That's supposed to scare them off."

"Let's get Ruth to sing," Angela suggested unkindly.

"Maybe I will!"

"What we should do is to make sure we stick together. No wandering off," said the Initiator firmly.

As if they would, thought Ruth. She had noticed already how closely the other nineteen stayed together, as if to make up in physical closeness for the waning power of the Web.

They stopped for a meal at noon and drank the small amount of water that they had carried with them from the last stream they had passed.

"Now we're committed," said Luke, with a tight smile. "We have to climb over the top of this ridge and down the other side to get more water."

They set out again in silence. The dark trees slipped by as they climbed. Their feet made no sound on a mulch of fallen pine needles. They stepped on fallen trees that fell apart into orange powder at their touch. It was very still.

They climbed doggedly on, longing to be clear of the

84

sombre trees, but it seemed that no matter how far they climbed the same trees loomed ahead of them.

"Luke, are you sure we're not going round in circles?"

"Will we really reach the river before nightfall?"

"We're climbing straight and we'll make it. According to the map the river's only fourteen kilometres from our last camp."

"On the map. The map's flat."

"I know. I've taken that into account. It *can't* be much farther."

Even Ruth's weak Esper power could detect the doubt in Luke's voice. She began to count her steps, as she had done in training back on Ark Three. Eighteen steps to a flight. Pause for breath on the landing. Eighteen steps up to the next. Eighteen times five makes ninety. No, the fifth floor had higher ceilings, didn't it? Ninety-six steps from the lowest level up to the Dome. Around the outside and down the next flight.

The problem was that it wasn't like that out here. Here you just climbed and climbed. She stopped, her hands pressed against her aching thighs. Then she gritted her teeth and began to count again. One, two, three ... ninety-five, ninety-six. And again.

There was a cry, and she looked up to see Luke silhouetted against the sky. He had reached the top. She could see sky and more sky, and it was suddenly easy to speed up and join him.

From the ridge where they stood they could see fold after fold of mountain, twisted and distorted by ancient forces and worn by time to smooth tops covered with the dark blanket of pine.

"We'll never climb over that, never!"

"We don't have to," Luke assured her. "We've already done the hardest part of the journey. Look down in the valley. Can you see that river?"

A white thread curling among the crumpled shapes. "Yes."

"That's our road. Along that valley."

"But that's not the way. It . . . " Ruth struggled with her feelings. "It feels all wrong. We shouldn't be going to the left."

"I know it takes us out of our way. But it's the only possible route. Two days up river, then over the watershed and down the other side, following the river southward that flows past Ark One."

"How many more days?"

"We're a bit slower than I'd expected. Perhaps six days' walking and two days' rest."

"Rest! When?"

"Tomorrow, if the Initiator agrees. Beside the river. Come on," he called to the others, who straggled up the hill behind them. "Downhill all the way now. But take care. You could sprain an ankle or worse if you start going too fast."

The descent to the river was very steep. By now, though the sky above was still light, the sun had disappeared behind the western range, and they found themselves descending into a pool of darkness. Slowly the pines gave way to birch, and then, as the steepness of the slope decreased, an occasional nut tree spread its broad limbs and made an open space for itself.

By the time they were within earshot of the river they could no longer see the way, and the Initiator called a halt.

"We'll make a fire in this open glade and pitch our tents while we can still see what we're doing. Luke and Ruth, will you go for water? But be careful. Don't get lost."

It was not hard to find the way, the river's voice was so loud. "See how white it shines, Luke! Oh, it nearly pulled the pail out of my hands."

"It's too fast. Much faster than I'd expected from the contours on the map."

"All that rain, I suppose."

"How are we going to get across? We'll never be able to steer the inflatable boat."

"Perhaps by tomorrow it'll have gone down a bit . . . "

They walked back through the trees with their load of water. The fire was like a signal, glimmering in the distance.

All through supper Luke was silent.

"What's the matter?"

"I should have thought about the rain. But we have to get across. We don't have enough food to wait until the waters go down, not more than one day."

"It'll be all right. We'll think of something. And it's not your fault, that's silly."

As she climbed into her sleeping bag that night Ruth suddenly realised that the advice she had given Luke was exactly what he had given to *her*. Her dreams had brought them here, but the choice had not been hers alone. It had been the community's. She curled up in her bag feeling as if a load had just slid off her shoulders.

She woke in the morning with the memory of a dream in which she had been searching the library for information on 'boats' and 'bridges'. No matter where she looked, volume B was missing. When she found it at last her hands had somehow got wound up in a ball of string and she couldn't turn the pages. It was a pleasure to wake up to sunshine and the song of birds.

Perhaps the river's gone down in the night, she thought as she went to wash, taking a pail with her for cooking water. But in daylight the speed of the current was even more terrifying. The water was a pale brown, with a foamy backwash where stones came close to the surface. She could see just how fiercely it tugged at the reeds and grasses that were almost submerged at the near edge.

How wide it was, flooding almost the whole narrow valley, nearly up to the base of that great nut tree on the farther shore. She filled the pail and then knelt to wash. It was surprisingly cold, considering that it was well into June. She shuddered and shook herself dry. Then she picked up the pail and hurried back to camp. I must tell Luke.

"I've talked to the Initiator," Luke said quietly, as they sat beside each other, eating breakfast. "Let's scout upstream when you've finished eating. Maybe there's a way . . . "

"Yes, of course. I'm nearly through."

As they left she saw Angela staring after them. "Do the others know how bad it is?"

"We haven't talked about it, but I'm sure they sense it. Why?"

"Nothing." What had she seen on Angela's face? It wasn't fear. It was more like hatred. "Nothing at all. Do you think we're likely to find a better crossing up here?"

"No, I don't. The river gets narrower, but you can see how deep it is and how steep the banks are."

"And since the same amount of water is going through as where it's all spread out, it's going to be that much stronger."

They walked back along the river's edge. "How on earth are we going to get across?" Luke muttered.

"Boats or bridges." Ruth remembered her irritating dream. "We've got a boat, but the water's too fast. What we need is . . . " She stopped and laughed.

"What is it?"

"It's silly. I was going to say string. It was in my dream. But why? Oh, I know! *Rope.* A piece of rope tied to the inflatable fore and aft. Someone on each bank holding the rope so the boat can't lose control in the current."

"Good so far. How are we going to get the rope across to the other side?"

"Throw it, with a rock around it maybe?"

"Hmm."

"No," said Ruth suddenly. "It won't work. You're going to have to have someone on the far bank to haul on the rope."

"Yes, and there's the last load, too. There'll be no one to hold the boat steady on this side."

"It was a stupid idea."

"Not, it wasn't. It was a great idea. We just haven't worked it all out yet. Go on thinking. I can see why the Four picked you to be an Innovator."

Ruth blushed and struggled with her idea. "Suppose you had a very long rope," she said after a while, "and you attached one end to the inflatable, then took the rope across the river and round that big tree over there. Then you brought it back and looped it round the trunk of a tree on *this* side, and tied the other end to the rear end of the inflatable, you'd have a continuous loop. That would take care of the last person across. Like this . . . " She scratched in the dirt with a twig. "It's almost like a rope bridge."

"It's terrific. You should get points towards your apprenticeship as an Innovator for this."

"You certainly should." The Initiator spoke from behind them. "Especially if you can think of a way of getting the rope across the river, around the tree trunk and back."

"PK," said Luke.

"Psychokinesis? Are you up to it? It's a great deal more complicated than anything you've done before."

"Ah, but I'll have Ruth to help me."

"Ruth? What have you two been up to?" The Initiator smiled.

"He's been helping me. But I can't do anything like *this*. Luke, be realistic."

"We'll be working together. And we'll have the others to help us. A little Web to give us extra power."

"Let's try. We've certainly got nothing to lose." The Initiator closed her eyes and concentrated for a minute. The other seventeen came hurrying down the slope to the river bank. Quickly the Initiator explained what had to be done.

I can't, thought Ruth. I'm not strong enough. Why me?

Stop that! The voice was so clear in her head that she looked up in surprise. Luke was frowning at her. How clear his thought had been! Maybe her Esper powers were getting stronger. Maybe she was more in control. Maybe it would be all right.

89

"We must hold hands, Ruth," Luke sat cross-legged on the ground. "With the others on either side of us, all linked together."

They linked hands, facing the turbulent water. Luke held Ruth's left hand. Angela held her right.

"Now, concentrate, everyone."

Ruth felt the strength of the Web flow through her body into Luke's. The rope lay coiled in front of them, one end securely fastened. She concentrated on the loose end. Slowly it lifted from the ground, wavered in the air, and then began to move slowly, snakelike, across the river.

She could feel the weight of it in her mind, sagging towards the hungry river. *If the current gets it we could never hold on*: the thought jumped into her mind. The rope sagged. She gasped and imagined it stiff, as stiff as an iron rod. For a few seconds she and Luke struggled. The rope stiffened and moved, coil after coil, across the river.

There was a low bough on the left side of the tree they had chosen on the farther shore. *Above that*, Ruth thought. Or had the idea come from Luke? It didn't matter. They worked as one. The rope looped over the bough.

"Take a rest," Luke said aloud. "I'll hold it for a minute."

Ruth put her head in her hands. It ached and felt as if it were swelling inside, pressing against the bones of her skull. She groaned.

"You're doing splendidly. Now listen. The next bit is going to be more difficult. We have to get the end of the rope around the trunk and back to the right side. You won't be able to see it, and that always makes PK more difficult. If you'll concentrate on keeping all this part of the rope rigid, I'll guide the limp end around the tree. Once we can get the tip around to the right side it'll be easy. All right?"

"Yes. Yes, I think so."

"Ready if you are."

Once more Ruth concentrated. There was a sledgehammer inside her head, pounding at the skull. All I have to do is to keep the rope stiff, she told herself. It's easier than lifting a pencil or a book off the floor, and I've done that lots of times. She could feel Luke's power tingle in her hand. Once he sighed and muttered, "It's like threading a needle blindfold."

There was the end of rope around the tree trunk! At the very instant of its reappearance Ruth felt a sudden jolt up her right arm and into her head. *You can't hold it!*

The rope sagged. She stiffened it at once, but the damage had been done. It was as if an invisible hand had tugged so that the free end had fallen back and flipped round and round the bough on the left hand side of the tree.

"Oh, Luke, I'm so sorry."

"Not your fault." He spoke between his teeth, his concentration amazingly unbroken. "I *heard* what happened. Keep the rope stiff, Ruth, and I'll try to unwind that end."

He struggled for what felt like hours, but at last he sighed. "Let go, Ruth, it's no good." At once the rope sagged and the river caught and tugged it. The far end held firm.

"Our only long rope," said Bryan regretfully. "What do we do now?"

"We'll untangle it, that's what!" Ruth jumped to her feet. She was furious with herself, and with whoever had jolted her concentration with that mean negative thought. She kicked off her boots and ran down to the edge of the water.

In a moment she was up to her knees. It was colder than she could believe, like being stabbed all over with sharp knives, and the current pushed her so that she staggered at each step.

The rope. That was Luke's voice in her mind. She saw that they had pulled the slack in so that the rope lay just above the surface of the water. She grasped it with her right hand and walked forwards, telling herself that now she was perfectly safe.

Just ahead was a smooth stretch of water, dark and free of foam. She walked towards it. The bottom suddenly fell away from under her and she stumbled forwards. The water closed over her head and she fought her way up, spluttering, her right hand clutching the rope so hard that she wondered if she would ever be able to loosen her grip.

The Web is whole again. The Web is holding you.

With a great effort of will Ruth stopped thinking about how *she* would manage, what *she* would do. The Web is holding me up, like a golden net. It is carrying me safely across, she told herself, and kicked and hauled herself across the river.

Something hit her right knee hard. Later on that's going to hurt, she thought vaguely. Now it was only a numb ache. She stumbled to her feet and staggered forward, still hanging on to the rope. Waist deep. Knee deep. Ankle deep.

Now she was ashore and turning to wave to the others. Then her knees gave and she had to stop and rub her legs before she could stagger over to the tree. The branch around which the rope had tangled itself was less than shoulder high. In a minute the knot was undone and she had walked around the tree and back to the water's edge. She tied the rope to her waist and looked at the water.

How cold it is. How deep. And now the rope is no longer taut, but lies slackly along the current. I can't go. I can't.

Nonsense, it's perfectly safe, she argued with herself. If they haul in the slack and let it out slowly as I cross I'll still be able to hold on. I can't possibly drown. It's easy. She forced herself ankle deep into the water.

But I'm so tired. The water's so cold and I have no energy left.

Come on, Ruth, you can do it. That was Luke's voice again. *We'll keep the rope taut for you.*

She waded forward, tripped and went under. She came up coughing and clutched at the rope. Death and the river, she thought over and over. Death and the river. I've done this before. In a dream.

As she clung to the rope the current tugged at her legs. She forced her legs to kick, her hands to move forward along the rope. Twenty-five centimetres. Kick. The other hand another twenty-five centimetres. Another kick. Until at last her eyes closed and her hands slipped from the rope.

7
Ark One

WHEN RUTH opened her eyes she was lying, wrapped in blankets, beside a blazing fire. She could feel its heat on her cheekbones, though her body shook with cold. Miriam, Paola, Grayle and Raef were busily rubbing her arms and legs. Slowly the numbness was replaced by a tingling, and the tingling by a throbbing.

"Oh, how it hurts!" she gasped.

"Thank goodness for that," said Miriam briskly and laughed at the expression on Ruth's face. "If you can feel pain there is no damage to the nerves. The pain won't last. Hold on. Soon you'll be warm."

I don't think I'll ever be warm, thought Ruth. Deep inside, where the fire and the Healers don't reach, is a lump of ice. But she was too tired to worry about why it was there. She drank a hot drink. The blankets were tucked around her and she was left to sleep.

She woke briefly for supper and instantly went back to sleep again. Next morning she was completely well except for this small nagging pain inside her. I suppose it's because I let Luke down, she thought, and pushed it out of her mind in the flurry of packing the tents and ferrying supplies across the river.

The boat worked splendidly, and after everything was safely on the farther bank they decided to leave it there for their return. "Then no one will have to go through what Ruth did for us," the Initiator said. Ruth felt a warm glow

94

at the implied praise, but then the sadness was back.

They made only ten kilometres that day, since most of the morning had been taken up in crossing the river, but on the sixth day they were off early, heading through the narrow valley between crumpled masses of tree-covered mountains.

The river seemed to have forced its way between these masses, which parted grudgingly for it, leaving only a narrow grassy strip on its south bank up which they were able to walk. As the day went on the path became steeper and the mountains crowded in on top of them. Even at noon they were almost always in shadow.

They walked silently, in single file. It seemed as if all the energy had been drained from them in the river crossing. Ruth saw the Initiator frown as she looked along the silent trudging line, and her face was anxious.

Before noon she called a halt. "Come on, let's unpack the fishing tackle and try our luck. Olga and Karol – you were the best. Let's see what you can do."

It was, as Karol remarked after fifteen minutes, like taking a biscuit from a baby. The river ran clean and deep and it had not been fished in over a hundred years. Before they had time to get impatient for lunch there was what Athena identified as brook trout in a pile on the shore.

Almost too beautiful to eat, thought Ruth, admiring the dark olive backs and the red-spotted sides.

"We're supposed to *eat* those?" Angela wrinkled her nose.

"You'll love them," said Ruth confidently, and when the Initiator laughed and handed her a knife she set to filleting and washing them.

They sizzled in the hot pan and gave off a most appetizing smell. Before long everyone was lining up with their plate ready, waiting for the next fish out of the pan. All except Angela.

"They're delicious, Angela," Ruth pleaded. "Do try one."

"How do you know, smart head? You haven't eaten yourself."

"Neither I have. That's easily remedied." She scooped a piece of delicate white flesh into her mouth. "It's even more wonderful than in my dreams," she said with her mouth full. "Come on, have one."

But Angela sniffed and walked away, down river. Ruth put the pan down and stood up.

"Don't." Luke put a hand on her arm.

"I've got to find out what's wrong." She ran along the riverbank. "Angela, wait for me."

"Why don't you leave me alone?"

"What's the matter? Can't I help?"

"You? That's a joke." Angela savagely threw a stone into the water.

"What do you mean?"

"You still don't understand? It was me who spoiled your concentration so the rope got tangled, crossing the river."

Ruth stared. *You can't hold it*! Not her thought, but Angela's. Yes, she had known it and had hidden the knowledge. That was the pain that had nagged her since yesterday. "But *why*? I thought we were friends now. Wasn't that why you came on the expedition?"

Angela's cheeks reddened. She threw another stone into the foaming river. "I ... I wasn't going to be left behind, while Faith and Charity got all the glory with you," she muttered at last. Then she turned away and burst into tears. "I never meant to endanger the expedition ... I thought I could keep my feelings hidden from the others. I did, too. I've always been strong that way. Only, down by the river ... Everyone holding their breath for you and Luke ... Your big PK act ... You never told *us* you had PK powers. Anyway my thoughts just slipped out."

"Angela, please don't cry. It's all right. It's over." She swallowed. "And I *do* understand. Sort of."

Angela turned on her. "You don't understand *anything*, stupid. Now everyone in the group knows how I feel. Knows what I did. Everyone."

"But they'll forgive you, too. It is all right, honestly."

"I don't *want* them to forgive me. I don't want them to *have* to forgive me. Don't you see? Oh, go away and leave me alone."

Then Ruth did see. To have been the top, the best, the star all the way from kindergarten. And now to be caught out in such an untogetherness . . . She walked slowly back to join the others and tried to finish her meal, but the once delicious fish tasted like shreds of synthetic.

The pan was cleaned and the fire doused with water from the river. Once more they set out. Angela had eaten nothing and walked slowly along at the rear of the line. Ruth felt a twinge – I shouldn't have left her alone. But it's what she wanted. If she refused to be friends what can I do?

She found she was walking faster and faster, putting as much distance as she could between herself and Angela, until she was at the head of the line. After all, she hasn't changed, she thought. She's always despised me. And she nursed her anger.

THE NARROW winding track, obviously made by animals, began to grow steeper. Beneath the sparse cover of grass and creeper the ground was slick. They had to watch their feet all the time. Now the mountain on their right crowded so close to the river that at times the path almost vanished. She wondered how the trees managed to keep a roothold on such a steep pitch.

She felt tense, so that her skin prickled and she wanted to scream. Her chest was heavy, as if she'd been running. It's being upset at Angela, she told herself. She wasn't used to being angry at people. I'll wait, she thought. Tell her I'm sorry and try to make things better between us.

She stood aside to let the others pass. Her chest was getting tighter. She could hardly breathe. Now her skin was crawling and the hair at the back of her neck stiffened. Something's going to happen. Something terrible . . .

97

The sun shone down on the river, though the path was in shade. It was quiet except for the voice of the water among the stones. She looked up, shaded her eyes against the sky. A tree, silhouetted darkly against the blue, trembled. How odd, she thought. There's no wind.

Stones rattled.

"Quickly!" Her voice was high with fear. "Run! Run, up the path. There's going to be a landslide."

She saw their pale faces upturned. They began to run, using their hands to help haul them up the steep path. Paola, Miriam, Grayle and Raef passed her. She counted on her fingers. Karol, Athena, Bryan. Charity and Faith. The Initiator and Luke. Eight more to go.

She heard a very faint sound, as if the earth had sighed. "Luke, help," she screamed. In a second he was beside her. "We've got to stop it."

He linked his hand through hers and they stood on the slope above the path, their wills binding the mass of wet clay that trembled on the bulge of the mountain above them.

"Gil, Basil, Helen." The Initiator's voice called out the names as the others hurried up the path. "Thomas, Crystal, Val, Olga."

Nineteen, she thought. Only nineteen.

"Angela, hurry!" The Initiator's voice was like a knife. "Run for your life. Come on! They can't hold on much longer."

The sulky expression on Angela's face turned to one of terror and she began to run, slipping and sliding on the twisting path.

Ruth felt her arms and legs shake. Sweat streamed down her face. Then Luke tightened his grip on her hand and whirled her round. They too were scrambling on hands and knees along the steep slope above the path, away from the river.

A single gust of wind, like an enormous sigh, blew up their hair. They turned in time to see the trees lean forward at an insane, impossible angle. Slowly, gracefully, they began to slide down the slope. Quietly at first. Then, with a grinding deafening roar trees, rocks and mud poured down the mountainside into the river.

The roar echoed up and down the valley. It was followed by a silence so profound that Ruth thought for an instant that she had gone deaf. Then she realised that the voice of the river, which had been with them constantly for the last two days, had been silenced. The path they had followed had been wiped out and a slump of boulders, splintered trees and mud filled the valley and held back the mountain torrent. Behind this natural dam the river rose slowly, brown and foamy. Before long there would be a lake where they stood. Later, perhaps, a waterfall. Where the bulge of hill had overhung the path was a reddish-brown gouge like a fresh bleeding wound.

Angela's sobs broke the silence.

"It's all right. Everyone's safe." Charity consoled her.

"It's not. Don't you understand? We're trapped. We'll never get back to Ark Three. Never."

"Nonsense," the Initiator said briskly. "Luke will find another way home. What concerns me more is that no one except Ruth seemed to guess what was going to happen. Why?"

"I was picking up a lot of negative noise," said Thomas, after a pause. "From the group," he added, and everyone's eyes went to Angela and then quickly flickered away.

"All right. We'll talk about that tonight. Luke, how far do we still have to go?"

Luke unfolded his map and spread it on a rock. "Another two hours' climbing should bring us to a good place."

"Can you all make it? Very well, let's go. No straggling please. Obviously the heavy rain caused that instability. It could happen again."

THEY MADE CAMP in a peaceful birch grove. They had left the river an hour ago and were travelling due east towards the

99

watershed beyond which flowed the great river that would lead them to Ark One.

In the darkness of firelight Ruth tried to reach towards the unknown. Surely by now she should have been able to contact the Espers in that other community. But there was nothing out there but the unease of the others and the shame of Angela.

And I must do something about that. Oh, what a mess we're in. And it's all my fault. Without those dreams we'd be safely home. If only . . .

"Stop it," said Luke, turning from the pot of soup he was stirring.

"I don't know what you mean."

He laughed and she blushed. "You're broadcasting so loudly I'm surprised you haven't deafened everyone."

She looked over her shoulder anxiously.

"No, it's all right. I think you and I and the Initiator are the only ones functioning normally out here. Even the Communicators are at a loss. But stop blaming yourself. Sooner or later we were going to have to face Outside. We couldn't go on living underground for ever."

After dinner the Initiator called them into a circle around the fire. "Our powers have weakened and I call upon all of you to strengthen the others. Fragmented we are weak and afraid. Together we can overcome fear and loneliness, as Luke and Ruth overcame the mountain. Join hands in loving and forgiveness. I call upon the Web . . ."

Behind her closed eyes Ruth saw the fire glow. From it spun a golden thread, as fragile as a spider's web. Around the circle it went, joining them together. Then it shivered and broke apart.

Me again, thought Ruth.

No. Luke spoke in her mind. *It is not your anger that is destroying us.*

Angela's face was in shadow. She turned her back on Ruth

and Luke and began to tidy up the camp site. Faith and Thomas began to squabble over whose turn it was to do the dishes.

Little things, but it shouldn't happen in a true Esper community, Ruth thought. Back in Ark Three they had felt so ready to build a new society, once the time was ripe. But would it ever be? Maybe the last hundred and forty years had been a waste of energy. "What do you think, Luke? Can we only function inside the Ark?"

"Like hot house plants? I don't know. Only time will tell if we can survive the frost."

With this bleak thought Ruth went to bed. It took her a long time to go to sleep, and when she finally did she thought she was still awake, because in her dream she was staring up into darkness.

Her dream hand reached out and felt for a latch. A door swung open and she felt against her face a gust of sweet cool air. But then she was back in the familiar nightmare, crossing a bridge over a raging river, knowing that the bridge was going to break – no, not break, but somehow tip her into the waters below.

She woke with a jolt and sat up. Had she yelled out? Apparently not. The other four lay still. She listened to their breathing for a while and then slid out of the tent, picking up her boots as she went.

The ground was noisy with leaves and twigs. She crept away from the tents and found herself in another glade, from which she could see the sky. The moon was up, a little more than half full, and she could see only the brightest stars. Ursa Major sprawled above her head. Arcturus cold and white. She had seen those stars in her dream, in the same parts of the sky. Somewhere, not far away, was a concrete bridge across a fast deep river . . .

She stared east towards the triangle of Vega, Deneb and Altair. *Tomi, do you hear me? I am here. We are coming.*

A breeze shivered through the trees. Suddenly, clearly in

101

her waking mind, she saw a face. It was the red-headed girl's. A word came to her mind . . . Rowan. Was the girl saying it? What did it mean? She felt for a minute warm and yet deeply sad. Then the feeling and the vision were gone as if someone had switched off a light.

At breakfast next day she asked, "What is a rowan, does anyone know?"

"It's a tree," Athena answered. "Of the order *Rosaceae*, with pinnate leaves and white flowers borne in umbels, followed by clusters of red berries. Sometimes known as Mountain Ash. Why?"

"I don't know. It just came to my mind."

The seventh day was a slow struggle up a brush-covered col between two mountains. Now they no longer followed the river there were no landmarks to guide them. Following Luke's map they had turned north-north-east, so that it seemed that they were getting further and further away from their destination. Halfway through the day they crossed another of the ancient roads and, just before they made camp for the night, they crossed a second. They both led south, over the crumpled mountains and down to the plain and the old cities that lay beyond. From this place they could look back down the long valley up which they had struggled for nearly three days.

"Let's camp here for the night."

"No," said the Initiator. "We will grow weaker if we look back. We must go on until we can see ahead."

They grumbled, as they would never have done a week earlier, but in the end they obeyed and trudged on. The grass grew wiry. A scatter of larch and birch were mixed with the dark of the pine.

Suddenly the land fell away from beneath their feet. They were looking down into an immensely wide valley. Far below, a thread of white between the trees was a river.

"That's it!" Luke's voice was so triumphant that Ruth knew that in spite of his calm he too had not been sure.

"Tomorrow we'll be down there. Maybe go a little way south."

Now they could see their destination they all became more cheerful. "Though it's taken longer than we counted on. We'd counted on reaching Ark One in a week. It's going to take us at least two more days."

"That long? But . . ."

"If we follow the river. That's the safest way, but it makes a big loop to the east here, before heading south."

"Will we have trouble crossing it?"

"We won't have to. Ark One's built on the west bank."

So why do I keep remembering the dream of the bridge? And why do I feel prickly again, instead of being as happy as the others? thought Ruth.

That night she crept out of the tent again to look up at the stars. Over to the southeast, that's where Ark One should be. Just below the tail of the Scorpion. The sting of the Scorpion.

We're so close. Why can't you talk to me, Tomi?

Suppose we walk for two more days and there is no Dome? But there has to be. It was on the map. Suppose we find a deserted city, the dome broken like an eggshell?

Then where do my dreams come from?

THE EIGHTH DAY brought new muscles into play as they began the steep descent to the river. But climbing down was much quicker than climbing up, and it was only noon when they reached it. They dropped their loads thankfully, stripped off their dusty clothes and bathed and washed their hair.

"We must look our best. I wonder if they're expecting us."

"Expecting us? I doubt it." Thomas shrugged. "We've reached out constantly to this new Ark, but all we get is silence."

"Yet their Esper signals reached Ruth a hundred kilometres and three mountain ranges away."

103

"It makes no sense, but there it is." Thomas spread his hands. "Silence."

"Keep trying," said the Initiator. "That's all you can do."

THAT NIGHT they camped close to the river, and on the following morning decided to save time by cutting over the hills in a southerly direction to where one of the old roads, marked on Luke's map, should help them on their way.

"It's uphill again."

"But we'll save at least a day. We're getting short of food for the return journey."

"Surely they'll feed us and give us supplies? After all, we're colleagues. Almost friends."

"A hundred and forty years ago we were. Maybe they've changed."

"Maybe *we* have."

They found the old road, running more or less south, and turned onto it thankfully. Easy walking, the open sky above, the sense that at last their destination was within reach, raised their spirits. They swung along at a good pace and Ruth found herself singing.

> "So the Freedom Man danced out of the Ark,
> And over the hills so shady,
> Into the light and out of the dark,
> To be with his red-haired lady."

Karol whistled along with her. "Do you know it?" she asked in surprise.

"Not your words. But the melody is very old indeed. It's got many names: *The Gypsy Love, The Whistling Irish Rover*, and so on."

"But it's mine. Out of my dreams. How *could* you know it?"

"It's a folk song, with the kind of catchy tune that gets remembered. And, I suppose, new words get put to it. Do you know other verses?"

Ruth sang all she could remember.

"Strange. I'd have guessed that it was a freedom song from the oppressed level of a class society."

"But that's not possible. The Arks aren't like that."

"No, of course not."

They walked on in silence up a steeply winding section of the old road.

"But it *is* curious," said Karol, a kilometre further on.

They reached the crest of the ridge shortly after noon. Someone, back in the Days of Oil, had widened the road at this point, and provided a kind of viewing platform with a waist high bannister. The stones had fallen and the concrete platform itself was fissured and overgrown with weeds. But it made a good resting place. They dropped their loads and stretched.

Covered with the inevitable pine, the mountain rose to a crest on their right. To the south-east, below the eroded edge of the platform, they could see the land fall dizzily away to a flood plain, wide and lushly green. Across it the river meandered in a wide lazy loop.

In every other direction were the mountains, round-topped, dark green, on and on as far as they could see. Ruth leaned perilously over the edge and followed the course of the river. After it looped back to the west it was forced into the narrows between two mountains. She lost it at last in a shadowy gorge.

She strained her eyes. What was that? Just this side of the steepest, most shadowy part of the gorge, the white thread of river seemed to thicken into a knot. It had a shadow. It was rounded.

"Down there," she yelled. "The Dome!"

The others crowded close. "Where?"

"Over there. See it?"

"It can't be far. Let's go. We'll reach it before dark"

"A real meal."

"And a hot shower."

105

"Another Web!" They looked at each other, smiles spreading over tired faces.

"No, no." Luke flapped his hands. "It's at least fifteen kilometres. For the last ten we won't have the road to help us."

"As to the Web," the Initiator cautioned. "We don't know whether they esper the way we do."

"But Ruth's dreams?"

"They show that some powerful force is working from within Ark One. But they may not mesh. There may be no Web, no understanding. The fact that Thomas and the other Communicators haven't received a single signal ..." Her voice trailed off. She shrugged.

But I can feel something, thought Ruth. A prickliness over her skin and that heavy feeling in her chest, like she had felt before the landslide ... Her skin crawled as if insects were running across it, and when a hand touched her shoulder she jumped and cried out.

"What is it?" asked the Initiator.

"I don't know. Something."

"Don't worry. It'll come clear. We trust you, Ruth."

Not all of you, thought Ruth. She looked at Angela, who was cheerfully bossing Charity and Faith, as she had in the old days. It's not only her. We argue and the air is painful with the sharp corners of our emotions. I think it was only the Web that made us one. We ourselves didn't grow or change. It was all the Web. Without it we are little better than the barbarians.

THE WORN ROAD looped to and fro down the mountain, so that they had, in the end, to walk twice as far as the map had led them to believe. It was almost dark before the pines gave way to beech and maple, the slope became much less steep and the road once more ran straight.

They built their evening fire in the middle of the road and pitched their tents in the long grass at its verge, where the ground was soft enough for tent pegs. They ate quickly and

106

crawled into their tents as soon as the meal was cleaned up. Tomorrow they would reach Ark One. Tomorrow they would meet the people who had been their friends in the days long ago.

8
Rowan

EARLY NEXT afternoon they again reached the river. It was hot and, though the pines cut out the sunlight, the air was filled with the smell of resin and pine needles. Slowly they became aware of a new sound. At first it was so faint that they didn't notice it, but as they walked it grew louder and louder until it filled the still air.

There, almost beneath their feet, was the river, running dark and deep between cleanly cut banks. Its surface was as smooth as synthetic, but when someone threw in a tree branch the water sucked it down with a swirl and it was gone.

They drew back from the power of the water and walked downstream, at a safe distance from it, through the dense pines. After ten minutes they could see that it was getting lighter. A new pale growth replaced the pines. Then, quite suddenly, there were no more trees at all, and right in front of them was the great Dome.

They ran forward and then hesitated. A wide concrete pad separated them from the Dome, and round its edge was a wire fence. Basil was the first there and he reached out to pull down the wire so that the others might climb over it.

"No!" The word was wrenched from Ruth's throat. Basil looked round in surprise, his hand outstretched. "There's something wrong," she went on, knowing, but not knowing why. The Dome was just like theirs. Yet it was different. Theirs was a dome of lightness, like a soap bubble. This one was a prison, lying in the forest like an ugly blister.

"Oh, what's that?" Charity pointed. A windblown rag? No, a piece of tattered fur. And over there a small pile of bones.

"A rabbit, I think," said Athena. "Nothing to worry about." She bent over the remains.

"The fence is electrified," Bryan shouted. "Athena, don't touch it!"

"Surely it wouldn't hurt a human being?"

"I wouldn't count on that."

"How dreadful. To think we might have ..."

"We had defences in the early days," Karol said gently. "Even guns, I believe. Though we never had to use them."

"But *now*. An electric fence still in use!"

"We mustn't prejudge these people," the Initiator said. "Let's look for an entrance. But carefully."

"Something is terribly wrong," said Ruth. "Let's not ..."

"We can't stop now we've come this far. We need rest and more food."

"There seems to be no door in the perimeter. There must be an underground entrance, like ours."

"It'll be hard to find in the trees."

"Let's walk around the outside. Perhaps they'll see us. It's strange that there should be no one here to welcome us. They must know by now that we're coming."

Halfway around the Dome the sun no longer shone on the plastic and they could see into the garden.

"There. Someone moved."

"Where? Are you sure?"

"Yes. He's seen us. He's coming closer."

Now they could all see the figure of a man, shaggy-haired and dressed in little better than rags. He waved at them.

They all waved back and cheered. The figure went on waving. Now he was jumping up and down.

"How very peculiar."

"He's not welcoming us," said Ruth suddenly. "Just see his hands. He's trying to make us go away."

"What a nerve!"

"No, it's a warning. Quick, hide."

From the safety of the long grass that crowded against the edge of the concrete pad they looked back. A second man had appeared behind the first, who had stopped waving. Now his hands were cupped over his head.

"He's beating him. How horrible!"

"We've got to do something."

"What *can* we do? Out here."

"It's all right. He's stopped now."

They saw the shaggy man scurry away into the green of the vines. The other leaned across the parapet to peer through the plastic. For a moment they saw him clearly.

"Sh! Don't move."

"He's gone now."

They straightened cautiously. "He was bald. Did you notice?"

"And there was something odd about him."

"He was a hunchback, just like the people in Ruth's dreams. What do you think? A mutant species?"

"Perhaps. But there's no good letting our imaginations run wild." The Initiator's voice was brisk. "Crystal and Karol, scout around to the right as far as you can. Olga and Bryan, go to the left. We'll wait for you back there, among the trees."

In less than twenty minutes the four had returned. "No way past," Olga reported. "The electric fence goes right down to the river, which has a high concrete embankment. There's a dam for the generators, but no entrance that we could see."

"Down river it's as bad," Crystal reported. "Beyond the concrete spillway there's a drop of twenty or thirty metres. The river comes over in a waterfall, deafening, incredible. No human being could get into the Dome from there."

"What'll we do?"

"Hunt for the other entrance. We're tired now. It won't seem so bad when we've eaten and rested."

As the others walked slowly back into the forest, looking

110

for a suitable place to make camp, Ruth suddenly felt she had to get away. She ran uphill, away from the Dome and the fear that seemed to spread from it like a dark sticky cloud. She ran until she was out of breath and had a stitch in her side. Then she dropped to the ground and looked about her.

She could see across the river, to a steep slope covered with scree and a few small bushes. Beyond the slope the land dipped and she knew – though how could she know? – that there was another river. And it was down *that* river that she must go. *This* was a prison. Down *that* river was freedom.

Is that really the place? She got to her feet, steadying herself against the coarse bark of a pine. Down in the southeast the land dropped away in a series of soft rolling hills. She saw another flash of river. Beyond it was the green of meadowland. Yes! She began to run back to the others.

SHE COULDN'T make them understand, not even Luke, and that was the hardest to bear.

"It's crazy to go all the way down the valley. You can see from here it's deserted."

"It's Ark One we came to contact. Ark One."

Ruth wrung her hands. "Please don't. It's dangerous. I know it is."

"At least explain."

"I can't. That's the problem. Look, let me go down there by myself. But wait for me. Rest for a day. Don't do anything rash."

"Ruth, that's crazy. There are people needing us inside this Ark – that man who was being beaten."

"Luke, I thought *you*'d understand."

"But you haven't told us anything we *can* understand."

"All right, everyone." The Initiator intervened. "We'll camp up river out of sight. Ruth can go down to this place in the morning. I'll go with her and Luke will be in charge here."

"Initiator, I must go tonight. I must."

"What's the hurry, Ruth? You need rest. We all do."

111

"I don't know." Rowan. The word jumped into Ruth's mind, but what was the use of it? A tree with white flowers and clusters of red berries. Why should it be so important?

"Then stay. Have a meal and sleep."

"I'm sorry. Let me go alone." She walked rapidly away again, with the others straggling behind her. Almost two kilometres up river the banks were closer together and there was a fallen tree half in the water, half out. Beyond it was a gap of about a metre to the farther shore.

"Yes!" Ruth ran recklessly along the mossy trunk and leapt. She slipped, grabbed at grass, at the exposed root of a tree, and then hauled herself out of the river's grasp.

The Initiator followed her, negotiating the jump neatly. "You don't have to come," Ruth said. "It's all right."

"Perhaps I want to." She turned to the others, clustered by the river bank. "Make camp back in the trees close by. We'll be back by evening tomorrow. Take care."

"You take care."

Ruth didn't wait. She began to run across the scrub-covered slope. It was now late afternoon. The sun slanted across the hills to her right. It was hot, and myriads of tiny flies rose out of the scrub as she passed and clouded her head. She battered them away and hurried breathlessly on.

"Ruth, wait."

She did not hear the Initiator's voice. Her heart was thumping against her chest and every breath hurt. But it didn't matter. She was escaping from . . . from something. She was going back to the village. Back to the mountain ash.

She came to the top of the slope. It was just as she had known it would be. There was the peaty river. There was the forest beyond, maple and nut and beech. And beyond it . . .

The Initiator caught up with her. "Slow down a bit."

"I must get there by sunset."

The sun had dropped behind the western mountains and the valley was drowned in shadow by the time she reached the river. She slid down a bank of reddish dirt and plunged into

112

the water. It was a warm river, friendly, no more than waist high at its deepest, with a gravel bar to walk on.

Once on the other side she began to run downhill, disregarding the water that ran from her pants and boots. The sky was a glory of pink and gold. It dimmed and the strengthening breeze was chill against her damp clothes. She shivered.

How tired I am. Surely it can't be much further?

The passion that had filled her and sent her headlong from Ark One was gone. She was cold and frightened. And it was getting dark.

"What am I doing here? Who has brought me?"

The forest did not answer. Somewhere over to her right the river chuckled softly, as if at some secret jest. She stopped, bewildered, and the Initiator's footsteps crunched on dead leaves behind her.

"Which way now, Ruth?"

"I don't know. You shouldn't have come. I'm lost. I don't know what I'm doing here."

"Hush. Don't panic. It'll be all right. Maybe we'd better stop here and rest till morning."

Ruth's shoulders slumped. "I suppose ..." Then she stiffened. "Over there, between the trees. A light. Oh, I was right after all."

She ran, her hands in front of her to protect her face. She bumped into trees, branches caught her clothes and hair. It didn't matter. She was going home towards the soft glow that was like a second sunset, but down there, in the east. She ran clear out of the trees and into the firelit glade before she could stop herself.

Shadows came together and scattered, resolving themselves into a group of strange — but not entirely strange — people. Their hair was long, they were dressed in furs, with their arms and legs bare. They had the look of people accustomed to the sun and wind.

She stood still and stared at them.

"Not a slave," a voice said.

"Nor a Lady. Look at her hair."

"And the clothes. The clothes of a stranger."

"Is that possible?"

The voices were not frightening, and Ruth did not draw back when they reached out to pull her close to the firelight. Many hands reached out curiously to touch her hair, her face, her clothes.

"My name is Ruth." Her voice was actually steady. "I come from . . . " She hesitated. What was this talk of slaves and ladies? For the sake of the others she had better be careful, at least until she knew more. "I come from over the hills, to the west. A ten days' journey."

There were exclamations of astonishment, and then a man stepped forward from the crowd. He had a good face, she thought, despite his shaggy hair and weatherbeaten look and the knife worn at his belt. "*Why* did you come?"

The question hung in the air. It was not one she could evade, but how could she possibly expect these people to understand or believe her tale of Esper powers and dreams? A little of the truth, perhaps.

"I think I was called. I am to meet someone."

"Who? Give us a name."

"I can't. I don't know it. But . . . I know this'll sound crazy, but it's something to do with a rowan tree. Perhaps I am supposed to meet them under a rowan. Is there one near here?"

There was a sudden stir at her words and whispers ran to and fro. Then the crowd parted and from among them stepped a young girl. She was about Ruth's age, with blue eyes and tanned skin. Her red hair flowed down her back, glinting gold and copper in the firelight.

Why, I know *you*, thought Ruth, in sudden excitement. It was the girl in her drawings, the girl whose memory haunted her dreams.

Now she was smiling and holding out her hand. "*I* am Rowan," she said.

114

9
The Sharing

"MY NAME is Rowan. But who are you? How do you know my name?"

"There is another." A man's voice interrupted. There was an urgency in his tone, though he spoke quietly, that made Ruth turn round. "There. In the shadow of the trees."

"Oh, that is the Initiator. We came together."

She waved and the Initiator walked across the glade, her hands held up and apart in a gesture of friendship. "We come in peace," she said formally. Then, with a little laugh. "And we are very hungry."

It was the right thing to say. There was a bustle, and hot soup and flat bread were produced. "This year we are growing wheat, but until it is ripe this is all we have to offer. Eat it. It is good, made from roots and pollen."

"You are very kind." The Initiator sat on the ground by the fire and began to eat. Ruth followed her example, though the closeness of the tall man with the knife in his belt and the other, whose folded arms were as thick and gnarled as tree trunks, made her uneasy.

As she ate, Ruth listened to the conversation of the strangers. Always close to Rowan was a young man with long brown hair and dark eyes but still beardless, called Arbor. The tall man with the knife was called Swift, and his wife, Healhand, was a woman with a calm strong face. The muscled man was Treefeller, and she guessed from the conversation that he was Arbor's father, and that Swift and

Healhand were the parents of Rowan and a mischievous boy called Groundsel.

Men and women alike wore their hair long, either loose about their shoulders or plaited and tied with leather thongs; and the men had beards, some, like the old man called Stargazer, white and straggling down their chests. They wore the rough fur tunics that she had seen in her dreams, and necklaces of dried berries or the claws of small animals, and in their hair were small bundles of birds' feathers.

As soon as the broth and the bread were finished the questions began. They were addressed mostly to the Initiator, and it soon became clear to Ruth that these people did not trust her. Swift was the main spokesman, asking over and over again every detail of life in Ark Three.

"And you're telling me that everyone works? Even the leaders? The ones you call the Four?"

"It's perfectly true," Ruth interrupted. "I've done the dishes alongside the Initiator or the Warden. Why, I believe that even the really dirty jobs, like cleaning out the purification tanks, are done by the grown-ups."

"You believe? You mean *they* tell you this – you don't know?"

"I was a neophyte until a few months ago. Only the adults did the heavy or dangerous work."

"Is it true?" The man called Stargazer suddenly spoke – for the first time. "Did you shovel muck down on Five?"

The Initiator laughed. "When it was my turn. The job had to be done. It wouldn't be fair for only a few people to do the unpleasant but necessary work. We shared it, as we share everything."

"Well then, I'd like to shake your hand, ma'am." Stargazer wrung her hand painfully hard, though Ruth noticed that the Initiator never winced. Then he looked round at the others. "Well, then," he said, as if his gesture had proved something.

Swift nodded, but Treefeller raised one mighty hand. "Wait. You say you come from a place called Ark Three. And

116

that the same folks built it as built Ark One. You'll be on the same side, then."

"I don't know about *sides*. We came from the same University. When the oil came to an end the different faculties planned the Arks together. But then each department, with families and friends who felt as they did, built their own city. There has been no contact in the hundred and forty years since."

"Why? If you were friends. If you worked together." Treefeller shook his head. "It doesn't sound reasonable."

"It was done deliberately. We felt that, if there was no contact, each Ark might develop some particular skill that might be useful in the new world. And if anything went wrong," she added, "the problem would not spread to the other foundations."

"And now? Why have you come *now*?"

The Initiator turned to Ruth. "It's your story."

Stumbling over her words Ruth tried to explain to the strangers everything that had happened in the last year.

" . . . and so we thought that the people of Ark One had developed Esper powers like us and were trying to get in touch . . . "

"Esper? What is Esper?" Swift interrupted.

"But . . . you must know. Isn't it you? Aren't you from Ark One? Did I come to the wrong . . . " She stopped at the expression on the faces around her. "What is it? What did I say?"

"*We're* asking the questions." Swift stood over her. His knife blade caught the dancing flames of the fire.

Ruth swallowed her fear. "I'm sorry." She tried to keep her voice steady. "What was it you wanted to know?"

"What is this 'Esper'?"

"The ability to develop special skills of the mind, so as to transmit thoughts and emotions and to receive and understand the thoughts and emotions of others." She quoted from the primary text. "There's a lot more to it, of course."

117

Swift threw back his head and laughed. "If you can read minds why did you have to ask us who we were or what we had to do with Ark One?"

The Initiator broke in to try and explain the years of practice that had gone to making the Web, of daily psychic exercises, and of their deprivation since they had left Ark Three.

"But if it only works when you are all together in your own city?" Healhand asked gently. "What use is this Esper skill? It seems to me that although you mean kindly your skills are of no more use Outside than those of the soldiers or slave-drivers."

"Soldiers? Slave-drivers? Are you talking about Ark One? Surely you're mistaken. Perhaps, if you are not from the Ark, you have misunderstood . . . "

A growling dissent stopped her in mid-sentence.

"We *are* from Ark One. We know what we are talking about."

"But . . . I don't understand . . . "

"Oh, remember – something Karol said about an oppressed society . . . "

Ruth and the Initiator stared bleakly at each other. Into Ruth's mind came the picture of the bald man with the hunch-back beating the other, his arm rising and falling . . .

Swift looked round the group and then spoke with sudden formality to Ruth and the Initiator. "If you are not too tired we would like you to take part in a Sharing. Sit and listen. You will learn the truth."

Healheand sent off some of the small children to bring firewood. Treefeller heaped it on the dying embers and a blaze roared up, scattering golden sparks into the darkened sky.

Without any signal the people linked hands and formed a great circle around the fire. They circled to the left and right in a simple dance that seemed to Ruth to be exactly right, as if she already knew every step of it.

As they danced they sang, and the tune too was familiar. It

was the melody that had been running through Ruth's mind for the last year, the tune that Karol had identified as *The Gypsy Lover*. Now the words, coming together, made a terrible kind of sense.

> "The Lords' whips cracked till our backs were sore
> And the Three-eyes watched us bleed,
> Till we swore we'd not work any more –
> Die or let's be freed.
>
> So the Freedom Man danced out of the Ark
> Over the hills so shady,
> Into the light and out of the dark,
> With his long-haired lady.
>
> Now we're free to think and free to grow
> Under the sky so blue
> Down in the fields where the flowers blow,
> Part of a world made new.
>
> Ay-di-doh, ay-di-doh dah-day
> Ay-di-doh, ay-di-day-dee.
> Now Devil-on-your-Back can't make you pay
> And your children will be free."

As the last words of the song died away on the still night air the dancers drew back from the fire and sat in a circle about it. In the brooding silence that followed, Ruth's eyes slid from face to face. What was going to happen? Each face looked as if it were carved from stone, or from the trees. The only movement was the flickering of the fire.

At length it was Swift who broke the silence. He began to tell the story of the End of Oil and the coming of the Age of Confusion. Another voice followed with the story of the Ark. It was similar to the story Ruth had learned in History, and yet it was different. This story was told stiffly, as if it had been memorized and handed down from generation to generation like a kind of myth, rather than something that was discussed in class and read about and that you had to write essays on.

119

Another voice added to the story, and then another. A fifth voice took up the thread. By now the blaze had died to a heap of glowing embers, by whose light Ruth could only dimly see the faces of the people. The story began to change.

"Then came a shameful night when a group of scientists decided in secret that it would be more 'useful' if they could spend all their energies on their studies, leaving those who were less successful or less powerful to do the menial work of the city. Thus was the community divided into Lords and workers. Already sockets had been grafted to the necks of both Lords and workers, sockets into which information packs could be plugged. The Lords gave themselves all the knowledge of the central computer, until their backs were bowed with the weight of the infopaks, but the workers were given only what they needed to function in their designated task and no more."

"How dreadful!" The exclamation burst from the Initiator. "Why did they accept such a life?"

"That was the terrible part about the new experiment. The infopaks taught the workers to be happy with their life, however boring it might actually be and however menial their tasks. It was a great success – at first. Then something went wrong. Some people's bodies rejected the implant that was necessary to connect the infopak. So these people were not like the workers. The computer could not force them to be happy. So what was to be done? They were both ignorant and free. Soldiers were trained by the computer to keep them in order and under control. Now this classless society had two more classes. Soldiers and slaves."

"How do you know so much about Ark One?"

"Haven't you guessed? You strangers with your Esper powers! We are the slaves who escaped from the city. From the stun guns of the soldiers and the whips of the Lords."

"You were all slaves?" The Initiator looked around the ring of people, shadowy in the dying firelight.

"Not all of us. Rowan, Groundsel, Arbor, and all the little

120

ones you see – they were born free. But for the rest of us the memory is still fresh. When we eat our food in freedom and breathe the clean air, we cannot forget those who are still inside. Our freedom is bitter."

The fire was a drift of white ash over a heap of red charcoal. Ruth saw the expression on the Initiator's face dimly, but she knew what she was thinking. That one of the Arks should have failed so completely! It hadn't preserved civilization at all. It had mirrored its worse excesses. Was she also wondering about the success of Ark Three? Into Ruth's mind came the voice of Healhand. 'What use is your Esper skill? No more use than the soldiers or slave-drivers.'

"We are very tired," she said at last, since the Initiator still did not speak. "Could we sleep and talk again in the morning?"

"Of course. There is always a spare hut, and enough furs to keep you warm." Healhand got to her feet and beckoned them to follow her.

Later, resting on a wooden bed heaped with furs, Ruth couldn't sleep in spite of her tiredness. The freedom song went round and round in her head. That's funny, she thought. There's a verse missing. One they didn't sing.

AFTER A breakfast of berries and flat cakes she asked Rowan about it.

"How funny you should know that. But you're quite right. Different slaves bring different parts of the song with them. Stargazer brought us one from the muck shovellers of level Five. I wonder if it was that."

Ruth sang the verse that had run through her mind all year.

"So the Freedom Man dreamed out of the Ark,
Over the hills so shady.
Into the light and out of the dark
To be with his red-haired lady.

121

It's like the one you sang last night, but a bit different. Why, whatever's the matter?"

Rowan was blushing. Her face and shoulders were flooded with colour. She looked up and her eyes shone. "You've seen him? Tomi?"

"No. Though I know his name . . . "

"Then where did you get that song?" She grabbed Ruth's arms as if she were about to shake her.

"Through my dreams . . . I dream of you often, but not as if I were Ruth, but as someone else . . . someone I think of as Tomi."

"I don't understand. How can this be? But I know you're telling true. No one has ever sung *that* verse before. It must be from inside his mind – Tomi's mind. Oh, how very strange. Come, you've got to tell the others."

"But I already explained about my dreams last night. What's so important . . . ?"

"We didn't really believe you. Did you expect us to? We thought it might be a trap."

"But you gave us food and a place to sleep . . . "

"Did you expect us to treat you as if we were soldiers? Or Lords? To be free is to risk. Now . . . what you've told me proves you were telling the truth last night. Come on."

Once more Ruth found herself explaining about her dreams. " . . . and there are two kinds. Some are just about life Outside, by the fire, or cultivating the fields, or hunting or fishing. I used to wake up from those dreams longing to get outside and be free. Oh, I just see what that song means: the Freedom Man dreamed out of the Ark."

Rowan nodded. "Go on."

"Well, the second kind of dream is far more real. It only happens now and then. Sometimes I'll get a new one – it's always close to the time of the full moon – isn't that strange? But then it may come back, the same dream, over and over. In those dreams I feel I'm another person, a man called Tomi, and it's his fear I experience. His fear, his loneliness."

122

There was a buzz of conversation. "Wait," cried Rowan. "Listen to her. It's all true. Don't you see, it has to be! We're ordinary people and all this talk of esper is over our heads. But I want to prove to you that Ruth is telling the truth. She says she only gets a new dream at the time of the full moon. I think it will also be true that there are five months when you had no dreams of that kind – the 'Tomi dreams'. The winter time between the Moon of No Squirrels and the Moon of Fresh Water."

"Five months. Between November and March. Yes, that's absolutely true. But, Rowan, how could you know that? Or was it just a guess?"

"In a way it was." She turned to the others. "Ruth dreamed true dreams through Tomi whenever he came Outside to bring us equipment too heavy to send down river. The plough, do you remember? And the big axe? And he only crossed the dam at the *full moon*."

"Yes," said Healhand. "The strangers have been telling us the truth. You've proved that, Rowan. But why is it so important to you?. You look – I don't know – all lit up today."

Rowan blushed. "It was the verse Ruth knew." She sang it. "Don't you see. Tomi's still dreaming about me, even though he knows . . ." She stopped and looked at Arbor. She bit her lip. "Arbor, I'm sorry. But I still love him. And if he dreams of me, such powerful dreams that all those days' march across the hills Ruth hears his dream . . ."

Healhand interrupted. "It's a hopeless dream, child. He's one of the Lords and you're the child of a free man."

"Healhand, he couldn't help being a Lord. After all, he loved freedom enough to go back to that place for our sakes."

"But you can never join him there. You wouldn't want to, even if it were possible."

"Maybe he'll come out again. Maybe he can help his own people out of that trap. Arbor, I'm so sorry," she said again. "I know I said I'd marry you next year. But I've thought about nobody but Tomi since he left. And now I know he feels the same way about me. I have to take my chance and wait for him."

"Good for you, girl." The old man Stargazer spoke. "The young 'un's for you, if you've the courage to risk for him."

Arbor shrugged and his mouth twisted into a half-smile. He turned and walked away into the forest.

"He'll be all right," said Treefeller, as Rowan looked anxiously after him. "I'm sorry not to have you as a daughter, child, but I respect your decision."

Ruth felt guilty at her dreams again. Now she had disrupted a happy community. Then she noticed a couple of girls of Rowan's age looking very pleased indeed, and she thought – well, he won't be lonely long. And he is very good-looking. She wondered what sort of person Tomi must be, that Rowan preferred him to Arbor.

"This man Tomi, the one I've dreamed about, you say he lives inside the Ark but comes out at the full moon? I don't understand. Is he one of you?" Ruth asked.

Everyone began talking at once, and it took quite a while to sort out the story of Tomi, the hero, the Freedom Man, who had once been a fat self-centred Lordling, but who had fallen into the river during a slave rebellion two years before, and had lived in the village for almost a year.

"He is a Lord, but not like the others. He came among us by accident. He was happy here." Rowan's eyes sparkled and she blinked.

"Then the saw broke and one of us remembered the great store room back in the Ark . . . "

"Full of seeds, it was, and all the equipment we would ever need to build a whole new world."

"Saws and hammers and nails . . . "

"And a plough," Ruth put in, afraid that they might go on for ever enumerating the wonders of the store room. "But why did he have to bring them out at night?"

"They'd kill him if they knew what he was doing."

124

"And us," someone else chimed in. "Kill us or take us back to slavery."

"So he went back to the Ark, pretending that he'd been lost for a year. And now he sends the things we need down river at the full moon. Or hauls them across the dam if they're too heavy to float."

"Like the plough." Ruth nodded. "I see."

"But this is wonderful!" the Initiator exclaimed. "Don't you see? We can meet this Tomi, have him show us the way in. We can meet the Lords as equals and talk to them about Ark Three. Perhaps we can persuade them to start a new life Outside."

"They won't listen. They'll kill you or turn you into slaves," Swift said definitely.

"I can't believe that. Not when they find out who we are. It's unthinkable."

"Think about it anyway." Treefeller leaned forward, his great hands clasped together. "Before you do anything rash, think about it. They are not like you, soft and gentle."

"Soft?" The Initiator flushed. "We made the journey across the hills. I think we could fight for our freedom if we had to."

"They'd crush you. They have the computer. And the soldiers. Two thousand soldiers."

"Two *thousand*!"

"Don't be in a hurry to make plans. Talk to Tomi. That is a good idea. See what he thinks. He has told us that he has been trying to undermine the work of the computer ever since he got back."

"How?"

"I don't know. But he has plans. You must ask him."

"On the night of the full moon? Is that when he comes Outside?"

"Often the night before. We go up usually on the night after the full moon to see if he has brought anything for us."

"So you don't always see him?"

"No. He has to be secret. We don't know the time of his coming or going."

"The moon will be full tomorrow," said Stargazer. "It rises early in the night."

"Then we should go up to Ark One today, shouldn't we? You can meet the other eighteen who came with us from Ark Three. Then we will wait for Tomi and make a plan."

THEY CROSSED the river and the col between the two mountains, and arrived in the dark forest shortly before sunset. Ten men and women came with them, among them Swift and Treefeller, Healhand, Arbor and Rowan. The others remained in the village, waiting for a signal, should they be needed.

"Don't we have to cross the river higher up?" Ruth whispered to Swift as they drew close to the great bulk of the Ark.

"No. See that great wall? It holds the river in its course. That building on top is a dam. The water goes down into a machine called a generator that makes the electricity to run the Ark. Do you understand?"

"Of course. Ark Three is built the same way, except that our river is a trickle compared with this."

"How strange it is to make heat and light out of water."

"That's funny. I never thought about it."

"But I suppose it is no stranger than people's minds meeting and exchanging ideas. I know the generator works. I must try to believe that your minds also work in a mysterious way."

"It would help." Ruth smiled. "But you didn't explain why we don't have to cross the river. How does Tomi leave the Ark to bring you things, like the plough?"

Swift hesitated. "It has been our secret for so long. But if I am to believe in you I must trust you. Across the top of the dam, over there, is a way down inside the Ark. It is to let workers come out and clear the grating of tree boughs and drowned animals, anything that might block the intake. That is the way Tomi leaves the Ark. He comes over the top of the dam and leaves the things we need out of sight among the trees."

Ruth nodded and stared at the dam. The sound of the water was deafening and the ground seemed to shake with its power. What must it be like to crawl across that concrete span in the dark, with the noise battering at one's body, dragging a plough? She shivered. It was her dream, of course. Not a bridge, but a dam. And she began to dream it at the full moon, when Tomi had to make his fearful trip. His fears had reached out and met her own and she had dreamed and redreamed them.

"But we are to stay over here," she explained to the Initiator. "So that means the others are on the wrong side. What should we do?"

"We won't worry about it until we've met this Tomi. He must know the proper way in – the underground route. And *it* will be on the other side of the river, that's obvious. No, it's probably all for the best that they're over there. But I must get in touch with them and let them know our plans. Ruth, help me make contact."

They sat with their backs against a tree and concentrated. Ruth was getting better at this. It seemed that as her tele-kinetic powers increased, so did her Esper faculties. It was too bad that the Warden hadn't worked that out back in Ark Three. She took a deep breath and let the sound of the river fade into the background. Her eyes shut and she joined the Initiator's mind.

They reached out and probed. And met nothing. Again they tried. And again.

"What's the matter? Is it me? Have I forgotten how?"

"No, it isn't." The Initiator scrambled to her feet. Ruth could see in the twilight that her face was very pale. "They've gone. Without leaving a psychic trace. I don't know where."

127

10
The Broken Web

RUTH STARED at the Initiator and felt a shiver run down her spine. Luke gone! "They can't have. Perhaps they're all asleep."

"I'd still sense their presence. But there's nothing at all."

"Maybe they got tired of waiting and decided to go back to your Ark," Swift suggested.

She shook her head. "They would never do that without waiting for us. And they couldn't have got that far. I should still be able to sense them. But there's nothing. Not a trace. It's as if . . ." Ruth saw her throat move as she swallowed. "As if they were dead."

"Do you think the soldiers came out and killed them?"

"No." Swift was definite. "The soldiers would never leave the Ark. It's not in their programme and they would be afraid to do anything like that on their own."

"Then where are they?"

"Inside the Ark." Ruth's voice cracked. "It's the only answer, isn't it?"

"I suppose." The Initiator ran her hand through her short blonde hair. "Luke was restless when I followed you. If he found the entrance to the underground passage and got tired of waiting . . . No, that wouldn't work."

"Why?"

"Because they couldn't unlock the door from outside. They could only have got in with help from inside the Ark. Tomi perhaps?"

Swift shook his head. "I don't think so. I have never heard of this passage you describe. If Tomi knew of it he would have used it to help slaves to escape."

"You're sure of that, Swift?"

"Wait a minute," Ruth interrupted. "Luke *could* unlock the door. He got the rope across the river. He held back the mudslide. The handle of the door would be nothing to him, if it was designed like ours – just a quarter turn, remember?"

"So you think they're inside the city?"

"They must be, mustn't they?" It has to be the truth, thought Ruth. The other possibility is just too horrible to think about. "Yes! That would account for the loss of their Esper signal, wouldn't it? Something inside the Dome is blocking it. That's why the communicators couldn't get any response before. Oh, that *has* to be it."

The moon had just risen and the huge Dome glinted icily white. There was something sinister about it. Ruth shivered and told herself not to be stupid. It was just a dome covering the garden, no different from their own.

"Perhaps it is the central computer," Swift suggested. "I don't understand this Esper of yours, but the computer is powerful enough to control the thoughts of everyone inside the Dome. Perhaps it is blocking the signals you think you should be getting."

"But the slaves are not controlled by the computer," Healhand put in. "They have no infopaks."

"And neither do we. So why . . .?"

"Perhaps our Esper is on the same wave length as the computer's signals, so that it somehow jams them. That would make sense, wouldn't it? Initiator, I just *know* they're not dead."

"All right, Ruth. Let's assume that all eighteen of them *are* inside Ark One. The next question is: Have they met the Overlord, the governors, whoever runs this city, and are they being treated as honoured guests? Or . . ."

129

"There ought to be someone out here to welcome us," said Ruth in a small voice. "If everything's all right."

There was a silence.

"So what do we do now?"

"Wait for Tomi," said Rowan practically.

"Of course! How silly I am being, worrying about things that may not even be happening. As soon as he comes he'll be able to tell us exactly what the situation is. When will that be?"

"Not until the moon is high over the dam. Crossing in the dark is too dangerous. But he might not come tonight. Maybe not until tomorrow."

It was maddeningly vague, but there was nothing they could do about it, except wait.

They camped among the trees, within sight of the dam, but out of sight of anyone within the Dome. "Though everyone sleeps at night," Swift said. "The slaves are drugged and the computer induces sleep in everyone else."

"But these are different times. It's as well to be careful," Healhand added.

They watched the moon slide slowly westward, occasionally veiled by a thin drift of cloud. The wind rose and it grew chilly. They huddled close, not daring to light a fire. At last the moon set and the stars blazed out. Pale owls drifted over the col. "He won't come now," said Swift. "We'll leave the forest and go down the hill, where we can light a fire and get warm."

They slept late, but the next day still seemed to last for ever. Ruth thought she had never seen the sun move so slowly across the sky. At dusk they put out their fire and moved into the forest.

Again the moon rose and lit the Dome. Again it climbed higher and shone upon the concrete path across the dam. They waited. The light moved off the dam, and the river and its embankments were in darkness again.

"He hasn't come."

130

"But he *always* comes. He was going to bring us . . ."

"Perhaps he can't. Perhaps the arrival of your people has changed what happens in the City."

"But in what way? We have to know what's happening. We can't leave our friends, but if we go in after them we may be walking into a trap," the Initiator said.

"If someone could sneak into the Ark and find out . . ." Ruth suggested hopefully.

"But even if we found the passage you speak of, the soldiers will be guarding it. The Three-eyes aren't stupid."

"What about Tomi's way?" Rowan suggested. "Across the dam and down into the Ark that way."

"They'd be caught at once. They wouldn't stand a chance."

"Suppose they pretended to be a slave? A slave with a message for Lord Tomi. It might work." There was silence and Rowan went on desperately. "I know it's a crazy idea, but it's better than sitting here waiting." Her voice trembled and Ruth realised that Rowan was as anxious about Tomi as she was about Luke.

"Well, I think it's worth trying," she said, and Rowan flashed her a grateful smile.

"What chance would any of us have to pass for a slave? Just look at us." Swift threw out his arm. "We're straight backed and sun tanned and well fed."

"I'd take the risk, Swift." The old man with the white beard spoke.

"Oh no, Stargazer. Even *you* look too healthy to be a slave. And what if they caught you, old friend? Back to another life-time of shovelling muck on level Five. After only a year of freedom? It's not to be thought of."

Ruth stared across the shadowy dam. She swallowed and all the terror of her dream was on her, the fear of heights, the sense of sliding, falling, being forced down down into the destroying waters. I can't, she thought. There must be someone else.

In the silence she heard her own voice, flat and unemotional. "I'll go. It's partly my responsibility anyway. It was my dreams . . . I'm skinnier than any of you and my skin's still quite pale."

"Ruth, you can't."

"Your hair's too short and what would you do for a uniform?"

"Yes, a slave's tunic. Without that you wouldn't stand a chance."

In the silence, Ruth let out a slow sigh of relief. She had done the necessary, the honourable thing. And now she was off the hook.

"What about Sweetgrass's tunic?" Arbor said suddenly. "You see," he explained to Ruth and the Initiator, "when an escaped slave is welcomed into the community we hold a ceremony and burn their slave tunic. But Sweetgrass only got away three weeks ago. We haven't had the ceremony. It would have been tonight. At the full moon."

Ruth managed a stiff smile. "I bet with a slave's tunic and my hair mussed up I could get away with it."

"It's still an awful risk."

"Less than if any of you went. I'm just a stranger – passing by. They'll know you're escaped slaves."

"But if they catch you, how would you explain away what you're wearing?"

"Oh, I'd think of something. I could say I found it thrown among the bushes and that my clothes were wet from crossing the river. I could think of something."

"Arbor, will you run to the village for the tunic." Rowan took his hands. He looked at her for a moment.

"I don't know why I do this. But . . . I'll be back at dawn." He kissed Rowan, and then was off like a rabbit, twisting to and fro among the bushes that covered the col.

"The rest of us should sleep while we can," Healhand suggested. "As soon as Arbor returns we will teach you how to behave like a slave." Her smile was crooked and there was pain in her eyes.

"You must keep your eyes on the floor all the time. Remember that, Ruth. It is very important. You are nobody. You are nothing."

Healhand's words echoed in Ruth's ears as she scrambled up the embankment wall above the dam and began to crawl along it. 'You are nothing.' If she were to slip now it wouldn't matter. She could catch hold of the bars that held back flotsam from the conduit into the Ark. It was once she reached the top of the dam that she would be in danger.

She crawled carefully along, the rough concrete painful against her bare knees. Here it was now, on her right. In the strong morning sun the water looked like a piece of synthetic drawn tight and smooth. Dark. Deep. And very fast.

She began the slow journey across the dam. She must not look down to the left. Swift had told her that. He had told her twice. Down there was a sheer drop to the rocks at the bottom, hidden from her by the spray that hung continuously in the air. The water poured through the sluice gates in a curve as smooth and hardlooking as steel. Down it poured.

She forced her eyes away. *You must not look.* She swallowed nausea and crawled forward. The noise of the falling water battered at her ears until her head spun and she felt dazed and stupid. Its force shook the solid concrete of the dam. What would it be like to be in that water?

No, don't think about it. Go on. Not far now. She stared ahead to where the concrete foundation of the City met the embankment. Across there the containing wall forked. One part joined the dam itself, the other joined the foundations. In the small triangle of shadow within the fork lay the secret entrance to the City. Tomi's way.

Come on. The path is a metre wide and no more than ten metres long. It's nothing. She inched forward, her knees scraping the concrete. Halfway now. Three quarters. She slid feet first into shadow and felt ground securely beneath her bare soles.

There should be a door and a latch. There. Her fingers

133

closed around it. She lifted the latch and pulled. The door swung open easily. Beyond was total darkness and the familiar smell of recycled air. She took one quick look up at the sunny sky, ducked her head and went down into darkness.

Her bare feet felt for and found the ladder she knew was there. Softly she felt her way down the rungs. Silently she groped for the latch in the door at the bottom. She cracked it open and a line of light blinded her briefly. The familiar sour-sweet smell of yeast drifted into her nostrils.

This Ark must be built after the same plan as Ark Three. There would be a stack of elevators at the centre, connecting the five floors below ground and the Dome garden above. But slaves were forbidden to use the elevators, except on special Lords' business. The rest of the time they were supposed to be invisible. If only she were! Nothing would suit her purpose better at this moment. She must find the stairs. How lucky that the training on Ark Three had involved stair-climbing. She knew just where they should be. *If* the plans were identical.

She eased the door open. The closest vat was fifteen metres or so away. Someone stood beside it reading numbers off an instrument panel and transferring them to a clipboard. His bald head shone in the glare of the overhead lights. He wore brown coveralls. He must be a worker then. They were supposed to be quite stupid. What she must beware of was the blue of the Lords and the red of the soldiers.

The room was orderly, bright and white. 'Keep to the shadow paths,' Stargazer had advised her. She looked to her right. About a hundred and fifty metres around the perimeter should be a door leading to the stairs. How could she get there unseen? The shadow paths? Not only must she avoid the bright pools of light that splashed onto the floor but, and this was more important, stay out of sight of the television monitors that must be scanning the huge laboratory. These, she had been told, were connected, via the Computer, to the infopaks of the soldiers, the Three-eyes, who were themselves

134

walking monitors, since they bore small video cameras on their foreheads.

She squinted up at the bright ceiling. There they were: a cluster of four cameras, each pointing in a different direction. An all-seeing computer connected to an all-seeing army. How could she and the others hope to outwit such odds? She closed the door and leaned against it, thankful for the sheltering darkness.

I can't go through with it. I just can't.

You can't let the others down either. Come on, Ruth. You've always wanted to be a useful part of the Web. Now's your chance.

Suppose they capture me? Maybe torture me with those horrible machines plugged into my neck like that poor worker over there?

Don't be stupid. The worst that could happen would be if they made you a slave. Then you could escape, just like Swift and Healhand. Come on, Ruth. Better to be a slave than go back across the dam to the others and say you can't do it.

All right then! She told the nagging voice in her head. Don't keep on so. I'm going.

She opened the door again and slid through, shutting it quietly behind her. Like a brown shadow she crept along the wall to her right. There were no other slaves in sight. Perhaps they normally had no business on this floor, which would be why Swift, on some Lords' business, was the only one to have found the secret way out.

Slowly she crept around the perimeter, never daring to take a short cut out of the hidden way, the shadow path. At last there was a door. She pulled it open and found herself in a different world.

Gone was the spotless polished floor, the air-conditioning, the brilliant light. Here, when lights had burned out no one had replaced them, so that pools of darkness disguised the piles of refuse in the corners and the dust and grit that lay heavily upon the landings and the stairs. There was a smell of unwashed humans and stale cooking.

She hesitated on the first step and grasped the railing, sticky with the hands of countless slaves. Two floors down, they had said. How could such a slum have been allowed? Weren't the people of Ark One committed to building a better world? Yet right in the middle of their model city was *this*. Well, at least she wasn't likely to meet a Lord or a soldier in these surroundings.

She had almost reached the bottom of the first flight when a figure came through the door and scurried past her, head bent. She reached out to clutch its arm. "I've got to see Seventy-Three. Can you tell me where to find her, please?"

The eyes were raised, surprised, fearful. "Who are you then?"

"My name's . . ." Ruth stopped, aware of the trap too late. She didn't have a name. Only a number. That was one of the 'privileges' of being a slave, that one did not even have a name. "Never mind. Just show me where I can find Seventy-Three." The other hesitated, crouching against the stair rail. "Oh, come on, you can see I'm not a Three-eyes, can't you?"

"All right then. I'll take you down and show you a place where you can wait for her. That's all."

"Thank you."

Again she caught a glimpse of shifting suspicion behind the pale eyes. Then the slave turned and trotted briskly down to the next floor, kicking refuse out of the way with hard bare feet. They emerged at the outer perimeter of the living quarters where, she had been told, the slaves slept. Ruth followed her guide at a trot around the long curved corridor and finally through one of many identical doors.

"Stay here. Someone'll come."

The door shut and Ruth looked about her. She had gathered from Swift that the population of Ark One was double that of Ark Three. But even with some overcrowding this room was repellent. It held five double cots. There were no closets, no

136

drawers. No place at all for personal belongings. To be a slave was not just to be a prisoner, but to own nothing, no name, no possessions, no history, no pride. They were herded like animals in an old-time zoo.

The floor had been swept and the bedding, though thread-bare, was relatively clean, but this far from the centre the air-exchange was not efficient, and the room had the sour hopeless smell of imprisoned humanity.

Ruth sat on the edge of a lower bunk to wait. It creaked dismally and sagged beneath her. It was very quiet out here, thirteen passages from the centre. There was no movement. No cheerful sound of voices.

Her brain felt tired and dragged down and inside her was a sadness, as if she were mourning for the death of a friend. What is the matter, she thought. Am I sick? Then . . . No, it's not me. It's the Web. It's completely gone. Not even the Initiator. I'm alone, really alone at last. Funny, I always thought I wanted that, when the Web crowded too close. But this . . .

It wasn't the peaceful emptiness of the Black Hole. There *was* something out there. It was like a continual inaudible hum, at the very limit of her brain's ability to catch it. After a while it began to be oppressive. A little while later it was almost unbearable.

It's the heartbeat of the computer, she thought. The great computer that runs everything in this Ark. She tried to shut it out by putting her hands over her ears, but it was not that kind of vibration. She jumped down from the bed and began to walk up and down.

I'll go mad if I can't stop it, she thought, and tried to block out the vibration with her own sounds.

> "Ay-do-doh, ay di-doh dah-day,
> Ay-di-doh, ay-di-day-dee.
> Now Devil-on-your-back can't make you pay
> And your children will be free."

Singing and talking to herself by turns, Ruth forgot her fear.

I won't give in. There's work to do.

I wish I were back home. I wish I'd never talked about my stupid dreams.

Don't be such a baby. It's no good wishing.

Why doesn't someone come? Where are the others? Where is Luke?

Luke. She stopped in the dead centre of the dingy room and realised that she was in love with Luke. It was the most extraordinary thing that had ever happened to her. It was as if she had been suddenly transported into the meadow outside Ark Three. She could smell the sweet summer grass and honey, she could feel the breeze against her face, the sun warm on her body.

"Luke." She said it aloud, testing the sound of his name against this startling new reality. "Luke."

The door crashed open. She was grasped by the shoulders and her head pushed roughly forward. A hard hand brushed across the back of her neck. She was turned around. "All right now. Who are you? Where d'you come from? What d'you want with us?"

This was a very different person from the scared youth she had met on the stair. This was a man, as Treefeller was, knotted and hardened by age and injury into something at last almost indestructible. An old laser burn across one cheek twisted his face into a mirthless grin.

She looked into cold grey eyes flecked with brown. She tried to keep her own steady. "My name is Ruth. I am from Ark Three – a place like this, but different. Far away. I'm here to find out about my friends. I want to get them out if they're imprisoned. And you too," she added.

He laughed, though his eyes were not amused. "*You* rescue us?"

She glared back, goaded by his mockery. "It has to start sometime, doesn't it? Though you wouldn't be the first to escape. To get away with it. You must know that."

Other men had crowded in behind the first. They filled the little room. In the silence that followed Ruth's last remark one of them began to sing under his breath.

"So the Freedom Man danced out of the Ark,
Singing, oh slaves, follow me.
Down the river of death to light or dark:
Either way you'll be free."

"Shut up." Scarface turned on the singer.

"There's no harm, is there?"

"You want the Three-eyes to hear about . . .?"

"About your freedom path?" Ruth interrupted. "You don't have to go that way any more. Not down the river of death. There's another way, a safe way. For all of you. If you want."

"What are you talking about?"

"It's too complicated to explain just now. Pleast trust me. There is another way out of this city, the way my friends came in."

"Then the soldiers'll know all about it."

"My friends wouldn't tell."

"You can't keep secrets from Three-eyes, not if they really wants to know," Scarface said grimly.

Ruth shivered. "You could check it out," she forced herself to go on. "Or don't you *want* to be free?"

A hand like a tree trunk was raised against her. She flinched but stood her ground. The arm fell and the big man laughed reluctantly. "You've got guts at least. But how do *you* know about a way out, when we don't?"

"Ark Three, our home, is built on the same plan as this. I'm sure we'll find the way out in the same place."

"It could be a trap, Eight-Forty-Two."

"Maybe. Maybe not."

Ruth clutched his arm. "Please believe me. Why would I risk coming in here, if I didn't want your good? And the good of my friends."

"What do you want then?"

"To talk to Seventy-Three."

"Why her? What d'you know about her?"

"That she's the Bentt family slave. That through her I can arrange a secret meeting with Tomi."

"The New Lord? It *is* a trap, Eight-Forty-Two."

Scarface caught Ruth by the chin and forced her face up so that her eyes met his. "What do you have to do with the Lords? With the son of the Overlord?"

"The Overlord? I don't know. I just want to meet Tomi, to give him a message from Outside."

"Go on!"

Ruth bit her lip. Should she tell them the whole truth about Tomi? Suppose they didn't believe her? They might get extra privileges by giving him away to the Overlord or the soldiers. The son of the Overlord. They should have *told* her. It was even more complicated than she had thought.

"Well?" The hand on her chin tightened.

"He's helping them – the escaped slaves – to build a community Outside. He'll help you, too.'

"A *Lord*?" He spat in her face and pushed her away so that she fell against the frame of a bed. She crouched against it, swallowing anger and nausea, wiping the spittle from her face over and over again.

"Watch her. Don't let her out of your sight." He spoke abruptly to one man and jerked his head to the others. In a moment the room was empty except for Ruth and one slave, standing stolidly against the door, picking his teeth.

11
The Lords

IT SEEMED that hours went by while the stolid slave stood, back against the door, staring at Ruth. She tried desperately to link her mind to Luke's, to the others, but she could feel nothing out there but the continuous numbing heartbeat of the city.

Perhaps I could distract him, she thought, looking around for something that she could knock over or throw with her mind. But there was nothing in the room. Anyway, where would I go? I have to be patient and talk to Tomi. It's the only way.

The door opened and a small woman slid through the opening, with Scarface close behind. Though she was obviously a slave, her tunic was neatly mended, and the dark hair that hung down below her shoulders was untangled and clean.

She stood in front of Ruth and stared at her suspiciously. Why, she's hardly any older than I am, Ruth thought, and wondered what it really must be like to be a slave, without family, possessions, learning, freedom.

"What do you want with my Lord Tomi?"

"You *are* Seventy-Three? Thank goodness! I thought you were never coming."

"What do you want with my Lord?" she asked again.

"I have to talk to him."

"Slaves do not talk to Lords."

"He'll talk to me. If you'll give him my message."

141

"I daren't. He might be angry. The Lords are all upset. Something . . . He could beat me. Or dismiss me."

It was clear from her face that this would be by far the worse calamity. Why, she's in love with Tomi! He must be something special, thought Ruth, though it complicates things. Can I trust her? I must. There's no one else.

She took the slave's hands in hers. They were rough and clammy. "Seventy-Three, it is vital for the safety of Lord Tomi, and the whole Ark, that you give him my message. Won't you do it, please?"

"What is it then?"

"I have to talk to him, somewhere safe and private. Say that Rowan sent me."

Seventy-Three nodded and turned to leave.

"Wait." Eight-Forty-Two stopped her at the door. "You can't bring him out here. If the Three-eyes find out they'll suspect another rising. Remember the last time?"

Seventy-Three bit her lip and frowned. "They're all over the Ark today. Trouble. Strangers, they say, from Outside, but . . . " She turned and looked more closely at Ruth. "You're not one of us. You're from out there, aren't you? You're one of *them*!" Her voice went up.

"Hush up, Seventy-Three. It's not your place to make decisions. The way you protect your young Lord I'd almost think you was soft on him."

Seventy-Three blushed up to the roots of her hair. She'll be in awful trouble if they notice, thought Ruth. She broke in loudly, talking to Scarface. "Surely there's a place where he goes when he doesn't want to be disturbed."

"Down on Four," Seventy-Three whispered, her eyes on the ground. "He spends a lot of time there."

"The storage area? Funny place for a Lord. But it might do. There are not many Three-eyes on Four. Find your young Lord and give him a message at once, Seventy-Three."

"Suppose he's in the library? He has a private room in there. I dursn't disturb him if he's there."

142

"You could send a note, couldn't you?"

"Who's to write it? I've forgotten how."

"I'll do it." Ruth's hand went automatically to her pantsuit pocket. "Bother. Give me a piece of paper and a pencil." No one moved. "Oh, come on! There must be some somewhere – if you have to steal it from a Lord!"

Eight-Forty-Two jerked his head and the slave who had been guarding the door slipped from the room. It seemed an age before he got back with a scrap of paper torn from the flyleaf of a book and a nub of pencil, roughly sharpened with a knife.

Message from Rowan, Ruth scribbled. *Meet me at your store room immediately.* She handed it to Seventy-Three, who tucked it into the belt of her tunic. "Do be quick."

"He won't come."

"He will. I know he will. Only hurry." She looked up at Scarface. "Would you have someone help me find the way to the store room?"

"Thought you knew this place like the back of your hand, the way you go on. There's dozens of store rooms."

"I know that. I mean the special one where Lord Tomi goes. I could lose him in the passages and get picked up by the soldiers."

"And you'd blab on us?"

"No, of course I wouldn't."

"Hmm. I'll take you down to Four myself and find a slave who's noticed where the Lord Tomi goes."

They scurried along the perimeter corridor to the stairway and down the gritty stairs. At the foot of the next flight Scarface left her. "Stay in the shadows there. If any slave asks what you're doing there, say 'It's Eight-Forty-Two's business.' Got that?" She nodded and he slipped through the door and was gone.

I wonder what time it is now, she thought. It was midmorning when I came into the Ark. It feels like the middle of the night. I'm so hungry. I wish ... oh, now I wish I hadn't thought about food. I'm thirsty, too. I suppose I couldn't ask them? No, they look as if they haven't even enough for themselves.

But water would be wonderful. Even recycled water. She found herself remembering the delicious taste of the water of the mountain streams Outside. If we do go out there to live, we'll drink that water every day. But why am I thinking about water? Where is Luke? Where are the others? Are *they* being fed and looked after? Or perhaps ... she remembered the slave in the Dome and the hand of the Lord rising and falling across his shoulders. She shut her eyes and shuddered.

"Come on. Are you asleep?" A skinny hand shook her arm. It was Seventy-Three. "Eight-Forty-Two said I was to take you. Lord Tomi will meet us in the South Quad, Sector B. Here, hold this." A heavy box was thrust into her hands. "If anyone asks, you're Ninety-Six and you're taking this to Lord Tomi. Got that?"

"Ninety-Six. Lord Tomi. Yes."

"Come on. No, not like that. Do you *want* to be picked up by the Three-eyes? Shuffle your feet along and keep your head down, your eyes on the ground all the time, but specially if you meet one of them. The Lords aren't so bad, well, most of them, but the Three-eyes ... "

"Seventy-Three, how can you *stand* it? Why don't you try to escape?"

"Hush. That's another thing. You talk too loud. And too often." She pushed open the door. "Come on."

They scurried down the great radial corridor that led from the perimeter towards the central elevator banks. 'Not many Three-eyes on Four?' Wasn't that what Scarface had said? They seemed to be everywhere, walking alertly along the main corridor, hovering in the side passages, stun guns at the ready, their heads turning this way and that. With their helmets and their central 'eye' in the middle of their forehead they reminded Ruth of the insects Outside.

She found herself flinching and scurrying by with shoulders

144

bent and eyes on the floor. Perhaps fear gave her the correct manner of a slave, for they were not stopped.

Suddenly Seventy-Three turned into one of the side passages. Allowing herself a quick furtive look Ruth saw that now their way was stopped by a Lord, a pudgy young man, bald and sallow-faced. 'The Lords aren't so bad, most of them.' Wasn't that what Seventy-Three had said?

He barred their way and there was nothing to do but stop. "Thank you, Seventy-Three. You may go. You there. Bring the box. You've kept me waiting long enough."

His voice was loud and contemptuous and Ruth felt her cheeks grow hot. She swallowed her anger and muttered, "Yes, Lord" in as submissive a voice as she could manage. She slipped into the room he indicated, noticing, out of the corner of her eye, an alert figure in red standing a few metres further along the passage.

The door slid shut and a hand, surprisingly hard in such a flabby body, was pressed over her mouth. "Say nothing," a voice whispered.

She nodded, her mind in a whirl. Was this fat pale stoop-shouldered Lord the famous Tomi? The man whom Rowan preferred to the handsome Arbor? She stared at him open-mouthed as he pulled from the nape of his neck a stack of information wafers. She had a glimpse of a plastic socket imbedded in the flesh, before the fold of his toga hid it again. She shuddered. How could they have done this to their bodies?

"All right." He laid the infopaks carefully on the shelf. "Now it's safe to talk. Oh, put that box down anywhere. It's not important. Who are you? You're not a slave and you're not from the village. I thought . . . from your note, that Rowan . . . "

He stopped and swallowed and she saw the pain in his eyes and the loneliness. She looked past the pudginess and the stoop and the baldness to the young man beneath, the one whom Rowan loved.

"I'm sorry. I had to make sure you'd pay attention. I didn't know ..." She stopped in confusion and began again. "Rowan is very well, and the others, too. Don't worry."

"Is she married yet?" The voice was very casual.

Ruth smiled. "To Arbor? No, I got the impression that the marriage was off." Her voice was equally casual.

"Oh? Oh, really?" She could feel the happiness radiating from him. It was almost embarrassing to be so close to a person's feelings. Close? She, Ruth, the worst Esper in Ark Three? How odd. Then she remembered: of course this Lord Tomi was no stranger. He was more even than a friend. Something like a twin. Even though they were meeting for the first time she knew his deepest hopes and fears. Here in the flesh was her dream half, her companion for the last year.

He went on talking and she pulled herself together to listen. "You're with the other strangers, aren't you? How did you get in? The way they came is now guarded."

"Across the dam."

"Brave girl. It still fills me with terror every time I cross it."

"I know," she said, without thinking. Then she couldn't help laughing at his expression. "I'll explain later. But why didn't you cross the river last night or the night before? It was the full moon and we were waiting."

"We?"

"Swift and Healhand and Rowan and the others."

"Rowan?"

"Yes."

He bit his lip. "So close." He seemed to be speaking to himself. Then he shrugged his shoulders and managed a smile. "I did not dare go out. There's been – well, the soldiers call it an invasion, but there were only eighteen of them. From another Ark, they kept saying. But, of course, you know all that if you're one of them. Anyway, the city has been in an uproar ever since. The soldiers are on edge, expecting more strangers to arrive."

146

"And what about the Lords?"

"The Lords! They've spent the days quarrelling over whether they should listen to the strangers or not."

"And the Overlord?" Your father, Ruth remembered.

"Ah." He looked at her without saying anything, as if wondering if he could confide in her. But in the end he said only, "The Overlord keeps his own council."

"So where are my friends? In prison, I suppose." Ruth managed to keep her voice steady.

"Locked up in a storage room. Not close to here, over in North D. But there are soldiers everywhere. That was why I was careful when we met. What a risk you took!"

"We had to find out what was going on. You see, the Initiator, she's our leader, and I went down to the village to meet Rowan and the others. We intended to meet you and decide on the best plan. But the others got impatient waiting – at least we guess that is what happened. When we got back to the Ark they were gone and we couldn't reach them. We had to talk to you to find out what was happening. We had hoped they'd be treated as honoured guests. After all, our ancestors were at the same University and we both started out with the same idea at the Time of Confusion . . . "

"Slow down a bit." Tomi ran his hand over the top of his head, as if he expected to find hair there. Ruth remembered that he had indeed spent a whole year in the village, living as they lived. "I'm sorry about your friends," Tomi went on. "The soldiers are trained to act first and think afterwards. They discovered them by the first floor elevators, and at first took them to be slaves – the hair, I suppose. They thought it was a start of another riot. Since the last riot slaves are forbidden ever to use the elevators."

"Were any of them hurt?"

"I believe they were only stunned. I'm not sure."

"You haven't *seen* them? I was counting on . . . "

"I'm sorry. I may be the son of the Overlord, but my position in the Ark is not such that . . . I am only a junior, one

147

of the Thousand. I had no authority to . . . Most of my time is spent in the library making new dreams."

"Dreaming?" Ruth didn't try to keep the contempt out of her voice.

He flushed. "No. *Making* dreams. I design the dreams that go into the computer and are used by the citizens. It is a way of keeping them contented. At least that was the original idea. I've changed it a bit."

Ruth suddenly understood. "Freedom. You've been giving them *freedom* dreams."

"Yes, but how did you know?"

"I dreamed them too. It was *your* dreams that brought us here. I'll explain when there's more time. But how very sneaky of you! We are on the same side, then. You and us. You will help, won't you?"

"I'm not sure what I can do. There's to be a full inquiry, of course . . ."

"You're afraid to do anything, aren't you? What does this place *do* to people? I can feel your fear – it's as bad as when they chucked you in the river."

He flushed. "What do you know about that?"

"I'm sorry. I shouldn't have . . . "

"You'd better go on, I think. If you want my help."

Ruth tried to explain about the Esper community of Ark Three. "And you've been part of my dreams since you came back. I think it must have been because of whatever you did to the dreams in the computer. I began to receive your dreams, so clearly . . . "

"You mean the ones I designed for Dreamland?"

"Yes, the freedom ones. But then I began to get you, too – your feelings, about falling in the river and being alone, and the dam and . . . and Rowan."

He flushed. "If you're so smart, what am I thinking now?"

She guessed. "That you want to help us?" Then she found herself saying, "And you want us to help you. But . . . I just came to get you to help us escape and go home."

"After you've come all this way?"

"We certainly don't want to stay and be part of this society."

"We came from the same place, you said so yourself."

"But your choice hasn't worked, has it? The computer and the information it contains has become the only meaning of life. Though I shouldn't talk. For us, the Web has become so important that we fall apart when it's not there. Back home the soldiers would never have caught us by surprise. Away from the Web we're useless."

"Let's try to combine our uselessnesses and break out of prison together."

"Do you mean it? Could we?"

"I think you've come at exactly the right moment. I've worked for a full year to shake people free of their fear of Outside through Dream Therapy. But it hasn't worked. I've seen workers and soldiers leave Dreamland full of ambitions that vanish into nothing. Until the next dream."

"Why? Your freedom dreams certainly shook me loose, and the whole of Ark Three, come to that." She laughed.

"The message the computer feeds into everyone's lifepak is so powerful that it overrides the strongest dream. It tells them that their job is the most satisfying in the world and doing it is the only thing that will make them happy. So the worker's job makes him secure, and the soldier knows that being a soldier is the finest thing in the world."

"What does it tell the Lords?"

"That their accumulated knowledge will make the world a better place. But not yet. Only when there is enough knowledge. But there will never be."

"So the City's a trap for everyone except the slaves. What do they think?"

"That life is hell and that anything would be better."

"Why don't they escape? More of them, I mean, than fifty out of a thousand."

"Because there are two soldiers to every slave, plugged into the alarm systems, the video cameras, the microphones. The soldiers hear and see and know everything that happens in the Ark."

"They don't know about me. Nor about your secret trips across the dam to take supplies to the villagers. Nor about what you have been doing to their dreams."

"You're quite right. You can see how that fear infects even me. But against the computer and the soldiers I can't fight – not alone."

"But with us to help! Tomi, why don't you just turn off the computer if it makes life so wretched for you all?"

"Do you think I haven't thought of that? Do you think I haven't challenged my father to find a way?"

"Your father . . . what did he say?"

"That there is a mechanism built into the computer that stops our interference with its special program."

"I wish I knew about computers. Are you sure that you can't find a way of reprogramming it so that the Lords and soldiers and workers start to think differently, so that they want to go Outside and begin a new life?"

"I've talked to my father about that . . . "

"The Overlord? You've talked about freedom? Does that mean that he's on our side?"

"It was he who gave me the Dream program. But it's not as simple as that. On our side? I don't know enough about him to be sure. I think so, but he is a confusing man. I only began to know him a year ago. Does that shock you?"

"No. On Ark Three the children are brought up in nurseries. Their parents are no more important than anyone else. The Web is our family, and loving and caring is shared among all. At least . . . "

"Doesn't it work out that way?"

"With most people. But I was awkward and difficult and I didn't fit into the mould. I used to dream about having a mother and father who loved me because I was me, not because I was a 'valuable addition to the Web'."

"I was brought up in a proper family unit." Tomi made a face. "The noble house of Bentt. Grandparents, parents, me. The one son, born to succeed."

"You just said you didn't know your father?"

"Nor did I. You can live in the same apartment as a person and never know him. Especially a person like my father."

"I hope I never have to meet him." Ruth shivered.

"Of course you must. We have to talk to him about the computer. Perhaps try again . . . "

"But won't he have me put in prison with the others?"

"Of course not. I don't think . . . " Tomi's voice trailed off, uncertain.

"Tomi, it's too much of a risk. If I'm caught I can't help my friends."

"But the computer is the heart of the matter. If *I* help you free your friends, will *you* talk to my father."

"All right. I do have an idea, just the glimmering of one. But to make it work we have to have Luke and the others. But especially Luke."

"All right. I promise I'll help. Now I'll go and talk to my father and work out a plan for freeing your friends. Wait here and don't open the door to anyone. Is that clear?"

She nodded as he slipped quietly out of the room. Only when the door had shut behind him did Ruth remember that she hadn't thought to ask him for something to eat and drink. She began to wander around the vast room, trying hard not to think of just how hungry and thirsty she was, nor of what the Overlord might say and do when he found out that yet another stranger was wandering around his city.

She looked at rip saws and fine steel needles, at the makings of a forge and of an operating theatre, at refrigerated units stacked with wheat and vegetable seeds. In this room was the source of the plough and the hoe, the green rows of growing things of her dreams. She had come full circle.

At last the door slid open again and Tomi entered, followed quickly by an older man, of imposing height despite the stoop of his shoulders, where a mighty pile of information wafers were stacked against the nape of his neck. The elaborately woven border of his robe proclaimed his importance, but it was his face that fascinated Ruth. Fascinated and repelled. His hairless face and bald head accentuated the height of his forehead, the beaky nose and thin lips and the hard stare of those sharp eyes.

Ruth stood like a child with her hands behind her back, feeling guilty under the Overlord's piercing stare.

"So you are Ruth?"

"Yes, my Lord." She found herself ducking into a sort of curtsey. "From Ark Three. Over the mountains to the west."

"It is extraordinary. Why do I have no knowledge of other arks? Why is it not in my infopaks?"

He glared so ferociously that Ruth found herself stammering, "I . . . I don't know, my Lord."

He ignored her remark. "You knew of us. You knew where we were?"

"We found maps in the archives."

"Computerized archives?"

"No. Papers and books. We have a very large library and an historical collection from the olden days."

"Don't you use computers?"

"Only for running the power plant and things like that."

"And your people are free?"

"Yes, of course." Ruth stopped, remembering the Web as perhaps a comfortable sort of prison. "Freer than you. We did come Outside. We did come here."

"Hmm. Tomi says you have an idea."

"Yes, sir."

"Well, go on. We don't have all day!"

"Tomi says there are some kind of devices built into the computer, things to stop you interfering in special areas."

"They were not built into the original design. But at the time . . . " He hesitated.

152

"I know about the Lords and the workers. What would happen if you did try to reprogram those areas?"

"I don't know. I just know that something would happen. Perhaps the computer would only destroy the operator. Perhaps the whole City. Perhaps itself."

"So your hands are tied unless you want to take that risk."

"Precisely."

"But ours aren't. I think we could help you, I really do."

"How do I know this isn't just a scheme to free your friends?"

"You don't, of course." She spoke boldly, though her knees were shaking. "But what could we do against your two thousand soldiers? Nineteen of us, my Lord, twenty with the Initiator. We need her, but she's still Outside."

He stared at her, his eyes cold and distant. Then she saw a muscle at the corner of his mouth twitch. She drew a breath of relief. For the moment, at least, she had won.

12
The Healing of the Arks

NIGHT FELL and the moon rose above the eastern range. Rowan and her friends took turns to sleep, while the others waited and watched.

Within Ark One the slaves stumbled off to their narrow beds in the crowded rooms at the perimeter of the city. The drug introduced into their evening meal took its usual effect and they slept.

In their separate quarters workers, soldiers and Lords prepared themselves for bed. Promptly at ten o'clock a stimulus in their lifepaks released a natural chemical into each person's brain. Soon they too were asleep.

STILL AWAKE were the eighteen from Ark Three. This was their third night as prisoners.

"I still cannot believe that these awful people came from our university, that they once shared our ideals," said Athena for the fourth or fifth time.

"Believe it," Karol answered grimly. "You've seen the slaves. You've felt the soldiers' guns in your back. Ruth's freedom song spoke the truth."

"Hate and love. The two opposites in the nature of human-kind . . ."

"These people may be hateful, but we in Ark Three were certainly not all that good." Angela's voice trembled. "We *talked* about a loving Web, but how loving were we to Ruth? How loving was I?"

"Don't." Miriam felt for Angela's hand in the darkness. "You know you're forgiven by Ruth. By everyone."

"Except myself. That's harder."

The crowded store room was dark and silent. Only the air conditioning whispered. Then someone shifted uneasily.

"It's I who should be asking forgiveness. If it hadn't been for me . . ."

"Now, Luke . . ."

". . . showing off my telekinetic powers, we wouldn't be in this mess."

"I just wish they'd work as well in here. Have you . . .?"

"Yes, of course I have. Over and over. I've no strength at all. Right now I couldn't bend a grass stem with my mind. I can't understand it . . ."

"We should sleep." Raef said softly. "Perhaps in the morning . . ."

"Let us try and make a Web once more," Thomas suggested, and in the darkness they linked hands and joined minds. A faint flicker ran like a golden bracelet around the room. It was strong enough to strengthen each of them with the surety of each other's caring love; but when they tried to reach out to Ruth and the Initiator it was like running into a blank wall.

"Sleep," said Raef again. "If they had been caught they would surely have been put in here with the rest of us. They are still free and we must trust them to do what they can for us."

ON THE SAME level, in a storage unit in South Quad, Ruth, Tomi and the Overlord were still awake. "What can your people do that I cannot?" the Overlord objected. "Why, you don't even utilize your own computer fully. How do you expect to understand ours?"

Ruth swallowed. The Overlord's piercing eyes seemed to scorn such alien ideas as Web making and telekinesis.

"I wish I were better at explaining. In Ark Three we are all trained in telepathy from infancy. I was different and so, I

155

guess, was Luke. I've only just begun to discover and develop my abilities, so I'm not very good. But Luke is an expert in telekinesis, that is moving objects at a distance without touching them, with only his mind acting on the molecules in the thing to be moved.''

"You think that your friend Luke could alter the circuits of the computer from within?"

How quickly he grasped the essentials. She nodded. "If you show him the diagrams and tell him exactly what has to be done, I'm sure he could do it."

The Overlord rubbed his hand across his face. He sighed. "I am still afraid that any attempt to meddle in the area I've shown you may result in the destruction of the computer. It is like trying to remove a tumour from deep in the medulla of a patient's brain. To excise the tumour risks ending the life of the patient."

"I *do* understand. I'm sure that if you explain exactly what you want to Luke he can change the circuitry within that area without touching the parts around it."

"You certainly have a lot of faith in your young friend. I hope it is justified. It is an amazing solution to what I've always thought was an impossible problem. My infopaks tell me that it may work. Logically it is the answer. Emotionally – I am afraid. So much depends on this young man, of whom I know nothing. Tomi, what do you think? Dare we risk it?"

"It's our only chance to break free, Father. For years you designed dreams about Outside, yet no one connected their dreams with reality and chose to leave the Ark – no one even wanted to leave. The dreams were a relief, nothing more."

"Have you had better success since I made you Dream Master?"

Tomi shook his bald head. "I have built into my dreams a longing for freedom and a sense of discontent, and I have based them on the reality I learned when I was Outside. But, although I walk about the Ark listening and watching, I have never heard a grumble. Workers and soldiers alike are content

156

to spend their lives as mindless servants. The control of the computer through our lifepaks is just too strong to break. If it were not for my memories of . . . of my friends outside, I think I, too, would succumb to its pressure." He sighed. "I've been wasting my time this last year."

"You certainly haven't," Ruth burst in. She blushed furiously when the Overlord turned his eagle eyes on her, but she went on. "I received your dreams. *I* wanted to be free, to discover the Outside. And because of your dreams we are here, from Ark Three, with the Esper skills you need to help you to free yourselves."

"Mind against machine. Will it work, I wonder? Will it?"

"It must, Father."

"Do you understand the consequences of failure, Tomi? It is an awesome responsibility." He sat brooding. Ruth opened her mouth. Tomi shook his head and she shut it again.

"Very well." The Overlord's hand slapped the table. "We will risk it all on this one chance." He smiled wrily. "I never thought I was a gambler."

DURING THE NEXT day a few people in Ark One were extremely busy, though for the rest life went on in its accustomed way. Secretly a message was passed among the slaves.

"Tonight we escape. Go to bed as usual. There will be no drug. Pretend to be asleep."

"Wait for Seventy-Three to come with the word and the way."

"Into the light and out of the dark . . ."

"At last!"

The murmur was passed from house slaves to cleaners, from kitchen skivvies to the muckshovellers down in the gloom of level Five. It was like a breeze that shivered the grass for an instant and then passed. Every slave heard the freedom words, but only the slaves.

But the Captain of the Ark's Guard was no fool. He was

Captain because he still had a natural instinct, over and above the computer information that bombarded his brain. The computer told him that all was well in the city, but his sixth sense brought him to the Overlord's office.

"What do you mean – trouble?"

"I can't say, my Lord. I just know. There's something in the air. Something big."

"Hmm. Any ideas about how to deal with it?"

"That's up to you, my Lord." The man stood stiffly in front of the Overlord's desk.

"Well, you usually know what you're talking about." The Overlord unlocked a drawer and drew out a small square package. "Make sure that this goes into the slaves' food tonight instead of the regular medication. *Instead*, remember, not as well as. We don't want a thousand poisoned slaves on our hands."

"This will do the trick?" The Captain weighed the package in his hand.

"It'll knock the ambition right out of them. And they'll sleep like babies. But it's strong, dangerous if it's used too often. You are sure that something's going on out at the perimeter?"

"As sure as I can be, my Lord."

"Very well. This will take care of the slaves for tonight. I will program your 'hunch' into the computer. Have your men at full alert tomorrow and we'll get to the bottom of this."

The Overlord nodded dismissal and the Captain clicked his heels, saluted and marched smartly from the room. The Overlord smiled a rare smile. How fortunate that the man should have come to him. So much more effective than having to send for him, as had been planned. As for the baking soda in the package, if any of the slaves complained about the taste of their food that evening, the soldiers would know that it was just the 'new medication'.

He returned to his study of the circuit diagrams of the computer, rehearsing in his mind the route to the heart of the lifepak program. As his fingers traced the lines he thought of what these diagrams represented: the life force of Ark One for a hundred and forty years.

A hundred and forty years ago a choice had been made – the wrong choice, the selfish choice – and the people of the city had paid a heavy price for it ever since. Perhaps more knowledge had amassed in a single place in the whole history of humankind – but at what cost! The loss of freedom of six generations of human beings.

Can the boy, Luke, reverse the consequences of that choice? The Overlord straightened his back painfully and sighed. He stared across the room, his grey eyes bleak, the lines from his flared nostrils to the tight corners of his lips very marked. Can Luke free us without destroying that store of knowledge, knowledge that we will need to start a new civilization Outside, knowledge that has already cost so much?

"What a choice," he muttered out loud and rubbed his dry hands over the tense muscles of his face. "What a choice for one person to have to make." Not for the first time he felt the intolerable pressure of being Overlord of Ark One.

WITH smooth precision the evening programme of the Ark proceeded. The eighteen prisoners received their meal from a different slave, a young woman who whispered, as she handed out their meagre ration. "Be ready. Do not sleep. Only pretend."

"Who sent you?" Thomas spoke under his breath.

"Ruth," she whispered back and left them.

A splutter of excitement was quickly quenched as Thomas said drily, "Eat up, everyone. If this is all we're going to get we may as well clean the plates and get some sleep. To-morrow will come all the quicker.

"Tomorrow?" Athena played up to him. "What is special about tomorrow? Oh, how long are they going to keep us here!"

They ate their bread and drank their water soberly enough,

159

but when their eyes caught each other's they could hardly keep the grins from spreading across their faces. Freedom!

In the Lords' dining room, in the huge hall of the soldiers and workers, and in the slaves' kitchen meals were consumed. Dishes were washed and tables scrubbed. In groups and singly the slaves straggled off to their quarters at the perimeter of level Three.

"PRISONERS all asleep," reported the soldier on duty.

"Everything quiet," said the soldiers who checked the slaves' quarters a little later. "Sleeping like babies.'

"All well," the Captain of the Guard reported to the Overlord.

"Was the new medication effective?"

"Seems to have worked like a dream, my Lord."

"Splendid. Your men may retire, Captain. Their sleep is programmed."

"I would still like to leave a guard at the entrance to the tunnel to Outside, my Lord."

"You really think that's necessary?"

"There may be more savages outside."

"All right. Six men be enough? Leave me their names."

The Captain saluted smartly, placed a list of names on the desk, turned on his heel and left.

Alone in his office the Overlord looked at the list of guards to remain on duty, ripped it across and tossed the pieces into his waste basket. The Captain would not know until it was too late that he had no intention of deleting the sleep program for these six guards from the computer. He glanced up at the clock. Nine-forty-five. In fifteen minutes the Ark would be asleep.

He walked down the empty corridor to the Central Computer, circuit diagrams in his hand. The door opened to his handprint. It was now nine-fifty. He looked around the familiar room. Here in this place was the accumulated knowledge of the world. In one small room. But then the genius of

160

Michelangelo, or of Einstein or Madame Curie were contained in braincases far far smaller. Perhaps after all the computer was not so great a miracle as the mind of the person who first thought of it.

Ten at last. He strode from the room and along the sleeping corridors of Ark One. He keyed open a particular storage area on level Four. As the door slid open Ruth jumped to her feet.

"Is it time at last?"

"Yes. Do you know what you must do?"

Ruth nodded. She slipped by him and ran down the corridor. She took the elevator up to the first level and hurried to the perimeter of the West Quad. There she stopped abruptly. On either side of the storage room, behind which was the passage to outside, stood a soldier.

Feet slightly apart, shoulders braced against each door jamb, heads bowed slightly over their guns, they looked like toys in their bright red uniforms. Ruth flattened herself behind a pillar and waited, her heart thumping.

What's wrong? They shouldn't be here.

The soldiers did not budge. She tiptoed over to a lab bench and picked up a pencil that was lying there. She balanced it on the edge of a petri dish and ran silently back to her hiding place. Then she concentrated on the pencil. After a few seconds it trembled, tipped and fell from the dish. It rolled to the edge of the table. She gave it a small mental nudge and it fell to the floor with a clatter that was surprisingly loud. Neither soldier budged.

All right, Ruth! She took a deep breath and stepped out from behind the pillar. She walked slowly towards the soldiers, expecting to see the guns whip up, to feel the blow of the stun against her body.

Now she was directly in front of the two soldiers and she could see that their eyes were closed, even though they were standing up. She took a deep breath and walked between them, opened the door and stepped into the room.

It was very much like the room in Ark Three that hid the

161

Door. Only there were four more soldiers inside, three leaning comfortably against the wall, the fourth collapsed in a heap on the floor. Ruth reached up to the bolt and forced it open. She was stronger now than she had been the first time she escaped from Ark Three, but the bolts still took all her strength. Luke's Esper powers were indeed impressive.

At last the door creaked open. She looked for and found the switch in the expected place and ran down the passage. It led straight on for about two hundred metres before coming to a dead end. There was the ladder going up to ground level.

She emerged from the passage in the middle of the forest and climbed over the concrete neck, which had been ingeniously disguised as a tree stump. How clever of Luke and the others to have found it!

She whistled softly a few bars from the Freedom Song. Within a minute a shadow appeared among the moonlit trees.

"Ruth? Is that you?"

"Yes."

"Thank goodness, she's here! Wait there, Ruth. We have to cross the river."

They appeared out of the darkness, Healhand and Swift, Stargazer and Treefeller, Arbor and Rowan and the Initiator. She was hugged by each of them in turn. It was strange. In spite of the danger and the dark she was happier than she had ever felt in her life before.

"Where have you *been*?"

"What took you so long?"

"Are the others safe?"

"How is Tomi?"

She answered the torrent of questions as best she could and then told them the plan. ". . . and Tomi says will you stay here, close to the exit, because in a short while all the slaves are going to leave the city."

"All? At once?" Healhand's voice was dismayed. "Food and shelter . . . thank goodness the weather is fine. I shall go back to the village and warn the others. We must prepare a hot meal. They'll be hungry and . . ."

"It's only for a couple of days, Healhand. Just to show the Lords and soldiers that the old ways are finished. Also . . ." Ruth's voice trembled and she swallowed and went on steadily. "What we have to do may be dangerous. Better if the slaves are safely outside. Later we can open the Ark so that those who wish to may come back freely."

"Peace, women," Swift broke in. "They'll be so glad to be free they won't care."

"Free or slave they still need food. Something for tonight. Tomorrow we can start building." She was off, plunging down the hill like an antelope.

"Start building," repeated Treefeller. He drew himself up and flexed his muscles. "That has a fine sound to it. We'll need more saws and axes, mind. Hammers and nails. Tell Tomi when you see him, Ruth. Then send out our friends. We are waiting."

"Yes, I will. Initiator, will you come inside with me, please. We have to get the others out of prison – they've been locked up all this time. Oh, that's not a problem. The guards are all asleep. The problem is going to be forming a Web to help Luke fix the computer and that's not going to be easy . . ."

"WE DON'T have long," the Overlord told them, when they had gathered together in the computer room. "The computer wakens the city at six in the morning. That is less than seven hours away. Whatever we do must be done by then. Once the soldiers wake and find the slaves gone the Captain will know I have tricked him."

Luke leaned over the table and traced the circuits with one finger. "Why do you not simply disconnect *this* area and then go in and change what must be changed?"

"Because to do so, my young friend, would be to kill the city. This area takes care of the ventilation, the generators and

163

therefore the electricity for lights, the elevators, the pumping of fresh water, the food processing plants and so on. Without these functions the city would die."

"Would that be such a bad thing?"

The Overlord stared at him bleakly. "In the long run it may be to the good. But tell me how to find food and shelter for twelve thousand people without preparation?"

Luke flushed. "I'm sorry. I just needed to know."

"Can you do it, Luke?" The Initiator looked at him anxiously.

"I don't know. I think so. It is a very different problem from moving large things outside me. To do this I must make my Esper self small enough to travel along the circuits within the boards and change what must be changed from within."

"It sounds dangerous."

"I don't know. We'll find out, won't we?" He smiled. "But I'll need help of all of you to make a Web. The interference is clouding my mind."

"But you can do it without damaging the memory of the computer?" The Overlord's face was drawn and anxious.

"I'm sure I won't damage it. I can't promise not to set off something that warns it. What'll happen if I do that?"

"I'm not sure. I believe that the early Lords may have built in some hidden defence system. Obviously it is not in the diagrams."

Luke whistled. The tension in the room grew.

"You still want me to try?"

The Overlord smiled mirthlessly. "I have decided that after all I am a gambler. Everything on this one throw. Don't let me down, Luke."

"I'll try not to. Form a Web around me, my friends. I will need every gram of strength."

He sat cross-legged with the circuit diagram on the floor in front of him. As he concentrated on it, the nineteen others formed a circle around him and joined hands.

Standing by the door, Tomi and his father saw the twenty

164

sitting with their eyes shut. The minutes flipped over. Five, then fifteen ... A faint hum began to grow and resonate through the room. Then a golden light, as faint as a sunbeam through mist, began to thicken in a circle above their heads.

Luke did not move. Nothing seemed to happen at all and Tomi wondered whether he had simply fallen asleep. Then he noticed the drops of sweat spring out on Luke's forehead, gather into larger drops and slowly trickle down his temples.

More time passed. The Overlord's eyes went to the clock. It was the only movement in the room. Tomi followed his eyes. Four o'clock. Only two hours left. In two hours the computer's wake-up signal would awaken the Ark. The soldiers would be alerted. The loss of the slaves would be discovered. The prisoners' empty room. They would look for the Overlord ...

Luke's voice made them jump. It was flat, the words dragged out as if he were talking in his sleep. "I have reached the gate. Now how can I go behind it? I can't hold it open with my mind and go on. But it mustn't close. That is what will destroy the computer. I need help. Ruth, come in and hold the gate for me."

"Luke, I can't. I'm not good enough."

"We've had a lot of practice. The rope. And the mudslide. You're going to have to stop being afraid, Ruth."

"Me? Afraid?"

"You're so afraid of your own power you won't let it happen. I need you, Ruth. Give yourself permission to be strong."

"All right. What must I do?"

"Put your hand in mine. Now come inside my mind."

Ruth took a deep breath and let go. It was painful at first, like being split in two. Half of her continued to sit quietly within the shining protection of the Web, of which she was still a part. The other half slipped like a shadow into the mind of Luke and became one with it.

"You see what I'm doing? Good. Just hold it that way."

165

"I have it, Luke."

"Keep it steady at all costs. If it slips the computer will be destroyed. Besides," there was a smile in his thoughts, "it's my only way back."

"Be careful." Like a vision seen through the wrong end of a telescope, Ruth saw a tiny Luke walk away from her down a long grey passage. The figure got smaller and smaller until at last she could see it no longer. Suppose he lost his way among the circuitry? Suppose he never came out again?

Her mind trembled with fear for him. She steadied it with a great effort. It required very little energy to hold open the gate, only a steadiness of purpose. Time passed. The gate was growing heavier. Years passed and the gate had all the weight of the world in it, all lying across her shoulders.

Ruth groaned and felt the strengthening touch of the Web. She drew it in hungrily and held up the weight of the Universe. Eons passed.

Tomi looked up at the clock. Five o'clock. A whole hour had passed since Luke had spoken and nothing had happened at all. Nobody had moved a muscle. Only the misty golden light seemed to sink down and rise again like a flame in a flicker of breeze.

The impersonal voice of the computer broke the silence with a suddenness that made both Tomi and the Overlord jump. "I am being attacked! I must defend myself. Leave the room immediately or you will be destroyed!"

"Father, what is it?"

"I don't know. I suspected a trap, but I don't know what it is."

"How can we warn the others without breaking that Web thing? If we do that Luke and Ruth will be trapped inside the circuits."

"We must wait and see what happens next." The Overlord's voice was calm. Only the twitching muscle in his cheek told Tomi of his tension.

"But . . ." Tomi bit his lip. His father was right.

The warning was repeated, in the same horrifyingly neutral tone. "Leave the room immediately or you will be destroyed."

"Look, Father! Down there."

From the circulation vents at the bottom of the main console drifted a thin tendril of green mist.

"Quickly, open the door. Poison gas! Use your toga to fan out the fumes. Like this." The Overlord stripped off his robe and flapped it to and fro. "Try not to breathe it in."

The golden light dimmed. "It's affecting them. If they should lose consciousness . . ."

"If we could only get in touch with them. If they could only hear us." The Overlord's eyes ran over the remote faces.

"Maybe they can. Ruth, Ruth, can you hear me?" Tomi knelt down, his face close to Ruth's. The green mist was acrid, choking; Ruth's face was smooth, shining with sweat. Then the lips moved clumsily, as if she were a statue speaking.

"Yes?"

"You must spare some of your energy to help us drive the gas out of the room."

"I can't."

"It's destroying the Web. Luke will be trapped."

"I . . . will . . . try."

"I will help." Tomi heard the Initiator's voice, though her lips did not even move. "I will give you extra energy. Together we can do it."

Tomi and the Overlord saw a small whirlwind suck the green vapour across the floor and out of the door. Little tendrils turned back, but they were sucked out. Before long the source had dried up and the room was clear.

The Overlord shut the door and leaned against it. "What next, I wonder?" he said under his breath.

Five-thirty.

167

RUTH CONCENTRATED on holding up the gate. She felt as if she were rooted to the ground like the trees of the forest, while her shoulders and arms, like great branches, bore the stupendous weight. "Luke, are you there?"

"I'm coming."

There he was, tiny, very far away, coming closer, getting larger, running towards her along the grey passage of the circuit board. Now he was beside her under the gate. Now he was past her.

"Come on, Ruth. I've done it. It's all right."

She could no longer hear him. She was trapped in the computer. She watched the grey walls recede as she seemed to grow smaller and smaller – or was the space around her growing larger and larger? Whichever it was she was now no larger than a grain of sand. Soon she would vanish entirely. But she had held the gate and Luke was safely through.

"Ruth!"

What was that?

"Ruth, Ruth!"

The unchanging grey light was suddenly charged with particles of shimmering gold. They danced, vibrated, came together in a pattern. It was a mesh in front of her. It was all around her pulling her backwards. She did not struggle within it. There was not enough left of her to struggle. She felt herself pulled gently backwards out of the greyness into . . .

Light? She opened her eyes. She was on the floor looking up at the anxious loving faces of her friends.

"We've done it," she heard Luke say. "You and I."

"And the computer is no more than that. Just a system to retain and retrieve knowledge, and a system to run the physical plant of Ark One." It was Tomi's voice. "No more infopaks. No instant knowledge. Or power. The Lords will be furious."

"They will learn to adapt. Soon they will be so busy sharing their knowledge on how to survive with the workers and soldiers that there will be no time for anger." That was the Overlord speaking. Ruth looked up at his smiling face and wondered that she had ever been afraid of him. That she had ever been afraid of anything.

A WEEK LATER she and Luke stood at the newly made entrance that now linked the Garden Dome to the outside. The electric fence was gone. Only a double door, built like an air lock, was there to protect the garden from the winter's cold.

Now, since it was summer, the door stood open. It was going to mean that butterflies and moths could fly in, and the gardeners would have to deal with this new problem of grubs and caterpillars. But, on the other hand, bees would take over the wearisome job of hand pollinating the peas and the tomatoes.

Hand in hand the two young Innovators stood, there to say goodbye to the eighteen who, rested and ready, were about to start out on the long trip back to Ark Three. Luke had given his maps to the Initiator and shown her the new route, due west down a high pass between mountains.

". . . and in two days' time you'll come to one of the old roads. It'll take you close to the big river. Follow the river northwards and you'll be back at the place where we left the boat."

"I hope the river's no higher."

"There may be less water than before. The mudslide may still be acting as a dam."

"And once we've crossed the river we'll be only three days away from home."

"Home!" The word was on all their lips.

The Initiator tucked the map safely into her breast pocket. "Are you sure you two want to stay here?"

"Of course," said Luke at once.

"And what about you, Ruth?"

"Oh, I'm half at home here already, knowing Rowan and Tomi. And how could I be lonely with Luke?"

"Can you really be happy away from the Web?" said Angela. "It isn't because of me, is it, Ruth? Because of the way I treated you?"

"Of course not, Angela. That's over. In the past. Stop worrying and learn to be a great teacher. I know you can – you were always the leader."

They looked at each other frankly, no more envy or anger between them, and moved together to hug.

"We will keep in touch." The Initiator kissed both Luke and Ruth goodbye. "We'll spread the Web across the days and the distance. We will never forget you."

Ruth blinked back unexpected tears and could say nothing. Luke's eyes sparkled with dreams of the future. "We'll boost Tomi's Dream Machine and use it to help keep in touch with you. Maybe with it we'll be able to find other Arks and link up with them. Then all of us, together, will begin to build. Roads and bridges to link us together."

"Maybe we can catch wild horses and tame them." Ruth smiled. "Then the distances will be nothing."

"Oh, how much I am learning from you two young ones," the Initiator exclaimed. "But that's the way it should be. We must go. May the Power protect you and the Web strengthen you. Goodbye." She left them and joined the others. They walked away from the Ark and in a moment or two were lost among the trees.

Ruth shivered and Luke's arm hugged her comfortably. "They'll be all right. They have my maps. They'll get home safely."

"Yes, I know. Just for a minute I was afraid. Everything is so new. There is so much to be done. We ought to go down and help Tomi. He's having a terrible time persuading those poor workers and soldiers that if they all take turns in the work of running the Ark, life will go so much more smoothly, and there'll still be plenty of time over for learning how to build a new world."

They took a last look at the dark forest that blanketed the

mountain to the west of Ark One. Then they went inside. As they walked along the gravel path towards the elevator stack, Ruth suddenly stopped.

"Oh, look, Luke!"

There, clinging to the pea vines, buzzing and blundering from flower to flower, was a honey bee.